Theia Thereafter

Volume I:

Chaos Emerges

Written by:

Waymond Wood

Cover designed by Getcovers

ISBN: 9798330495894

1st Edition

Published by Theian Mythology & Other Sci-Fi Publishing (independent)
waymondwood.com

Table of Contents

Chapter 1: The Arrival

The viewport glass was cold against my forehead. Below us, a massive sphere of bruised blue and sprawling green hung suspended in the void. Our ancestral home.

Chaos didn't smile. His jaw clenched tight enough to snap bone, his fingers rigid over the Arkenon's telemetry console. “We made it. These match the archive coordinates, but…” He tapped a holographic display, the blue light reflecting in his dark eyes. “Atmospheric density is wrong. It’s too heavy.”

I leaned closer. I didn’t need to read the nitrogen and oxygen ratios flashing in red; I could feel the planet’s erratic hum bleeding through the ship’s hull. The readouts spiked and dipped in a rhythmic, violent pulse.

"It's not just dense…," Chaos murmured. "It's breathing."

He swiped the holograms, isolating a cluster of pulsing white nodes on the western landmass and coastal shallows.

"Theian energy," I breathed, the syllables catching in my throat. The tiny ember of hope we had carried across the cold dark of space flared into a desperate fire. "So it is our world."

"It's a world," Chaos corrected, his hand hovering over the descent thrusters. "Let's see if it welcomes us."

The Arkenon shuddered violently as we pierced the exosphere. I stepped out onto the observation deck, the wind immediately whipping my crimson braid into a frenzy. Below us lay an ocean of endless turquoise bleeding into a continent of suffocating emerald rainforests.

But this wasn't the peaceful paradise of the elders' stories. A low, guttural roar rattled the deck plating beneath my boots. Looking down, the scale of the violence below came into terrifying focus.

Suddenly, a shadow passed over me. The hairs on the back of my neck stood straight up. The ambient air pressure on the deck dropped to a suffocating chill.

Someone else was standing behind us.

I spun, scanning the metallic platform, my peripheral vision catching a blur of movement that defied the ship's sensors. Beside me, Chaos's hand had already blurred to the hilt of his sword, his posture dropping into a lethal crouch.

Nothing. Just the howling wind.

Chaos slowly straightened, though his grip on the hilt remained white-knuckled. “Quite a view,” he deflected, his eyes still scanning the empty corners of the deck.

“Yes,” I lied, my pulse hammering in my ears as I forced myself to look back over the railing.

As we dropped lower, the clouds parted to reveal the true lords of this world. Leviathans with bodies like moss-covered mountains waded through the marshlands. Their massive, redwood-thick legs churned the earth into craters, their passage snapping ancient trees like dry twigs. Their whip-like tails carved deep trenches into the underbrush. We weren't returning as conquerors. We were trespassers in a kingdom of giants.

The Arkenon's landing gear slammed into the muddy earth with a heavy, metallic groan.

"No signs of civilization," Chaos growled over the engine's whine. "Just wild things that only know how to kill or be killed."

"Curious life," I noted, watching the treeline.

"Dumb, arrogant beasts," he shot back. "They have no fear. They think they sit at the top of the food chain."

I smirked, glancing over my shoulder. "Sounds a lot like Theia to me."

The ramp lowered, bleeding harsh, unfiltered sunlight into the cargo bay. They were already waiting for us.

Not the lumbering giants from the marsh, but bipedal hunters. Lean, feathered, and vibrating with hyper-kinetic energy. Their elongated snouts parted, releasing a chorus of piercing, rhythmic hisses. When they shifted, their feathered wings flared like rudders, twitching with predatory anticipation.

I stepped down the ramp. They tensed, their muscles coiling like springs.

I didn't draw a weapon. I simply threw my arms wide and let the power loose.

A blinding, localized supernova erupted from my palms. The accompanying sonic boom cracked like thunder, ripping through the clearing. The hunters scrambled backward, their hisses turning into high-pitched screeches as the shockwave flattened the tall grass. They didn't run, but they bowed low, their predatory arrogance instantly replaced by cautious, nervous pacing.

Chaos strolled down the ramp behind me, his boots heavy against the metal, swaggering into the sunlight.

"You see," I called back to him, keeping my eyes locked on the pack. "Resolution without bloodshed."

"Sure," Chaos chuckled, rolling his shoulders. "But my way is more fun."

"It doesn't always have to be total annihilation," I mocked.

"That only happens when I get angry."

"Need I mention… you always get angry."

The ground didn't just tremble. It buckled.

The aftershock of my sonic boom hadn't faded. It deepened. The vibration traveled up through the soles of my boots, resonating in my marrow. It wasn't an echo of my power. It was a response.

The bedrock groaned, then violently gave way. A jagged fissure tore through the valley floor, swallowing the screeching raptors into absolute darkness. From the rupture, the earth boiled upward. Jagged plates of magma-streaked basalt hooked onto the crumbling ledge. A colossal, segmented tail breached the canopy, dripping with molten slag. When it screamed, the sheer acoustic force flattened the nearest tree line.

The sun vanished. A living eclipse blotted out the light, casting a suffocating shadow over the valley. The air grew instantly, blisteringly hot. My lungs seized. I couldn't command my legs to step back. I could only stare upward at the fiery, molten eyes locking onto us.

"Umm… Brah…" I choked out, the syllables scraping against my dry throat.

Beside me, the air warped. Chaos didn't retreat. His aura bled into the physical realm as he planted his boots, digging into the dirt. "I think you woke it up. So... my way?"

"Yeah," I gasped, the heat stinging my eyes. "Your way."

The beast crashed into him with the kinetic weight of a falling meteor. The impact triggered a shockwave that kicked up a blinding wall of dirt. Through the dust, Chaos was being driven backward, his heels carving deep trenches into the soil, his bare hands locked desperately against the beast's snapping pincers. Above him, the molten stinger coiled, seeking a blind spot.

We couldn't match its mass. My eyes darted from the crushing pincers to the jagged, unstable rim of the newly formed chasm.

"Chaos! The fracture!" I screamed over the roar of breaking stone.

He didn't need to look. He understood.

I didn't run; I became a beacon. I slammed my heel into the bedrock, pulsing a concentrated shockwave directly into the planet's crust. Thud. The beast's molten eyes snapped toward me. Thud. I danced backward, skirting the very edge of the abyss, weaving a trail of seismic taunts.

Umbra surged, discarding Chaos to lunge at me.

I waited until the heat of its jaws threatened to singe my face, then I dropped to my knees and drove both palms into the fault line. The earth convulsed. The unstable ledge shattered outward, turning solid ground into a landslide. Umbra shrieked, its massive weight pulling it off balance, its magma-slick claws desperately scraping against the eroding precipice as it fell into the void.

Chapter 2: A Cliffhanger

The chasm edge crumbled as Umbra's molten claws hooked back over the rim. My breath tore through my lungs in ragged, shallow gasps. The gravity of this world felt like lead in my blood, pulling at my exhausted muscles. My knees trembled. We had thrown the earth itself at this beast, and it was still climbing.

There was no plan left. I pushed off my back foot, forcing my burning thighs into a dead sprint along the precipice.

The ground bucked behind me. Crash. The heat of Umbra's jaws scorched the air inches from my spine. Crash. The sheer acoustic force of its bellows threatened to rupture my eardrums. The jagged maw of the chasm opened before me, offering nowhere else to run. I didn't slow down. I spun on my heel, bracing for an impact I knew I couldn't survive.

Through the smoke, a blur of motion caught my eye. Chaos. He was back on his feet, but his scabbard hung empty, the strap shredded from the initial clash. I watched him scramble through the debris, his hands frantically tearing at the dirt until he seized something—a weathered staff, half-buried in the bedrock.

Umbra reared back, its massive pincers eclipsing the sky, ready to snap me in half.

Before the blow could land, the air pressure fractured. Chaos slammed into the dirt between us, driving the base of the ancient staff into the stone to break his sliding momentum.

The reaction was instantaneous.

It wasn't magic; it was raw, uncalibrated technology. The staff didn't just glow—it tore the atmosphere open. A concussive wave of violet energy ruptured outward, ionizing the air and tasting sharply of ozone. A swirling, violent vortex ripped into existence, gravity folding in on itself. Umbra's furious screech warped into a distorted gurgle as the spatial tear latched onto its massive frame.

I threw myself backward into the dirt as the beast's claws scraped the rim one last time. With a sickening crack of displaced air, Umbra was sucked into the void. The portal snapped shut, leaving behind nothing but the smell of burnt copper and scorched earth.

The sudden silence was heavier than the roars. The wind whipped my crimson braid across my face, carrying the bitter chill of the altitude. I dragged myself to the edge of the newly formed crevasse, watching groundwater already beginning to bleed into the massive scar we had carved into the valley.

I slumped onto the dirt, my chest heaving. "I thought we were done," I rasped, wiping sweat and ash from my forehead. I stared at the staff in his hand. "How did you do that? What is that?"

Chaos let out a ragged breath, leaning heavily on the weathered wood. "My sword was gone. I saw this sticking out of the bedrock. When I grabbed it... it hummed." He kicked at a loose stone, watching it tumble into the abyss. "I just wanted to get its attention. The staff did the rest."

"Where did it send it?"

Chaos spotted his sword half-buried in the rubble nearby and yanked it free. "Somewhere lucky," he smirked, though the bravado didn't quite reach his eyes. He tossed the staff toward me. "Here. You're the one who likes playing with local frequencies. See if you can channel your energy through it without blowing us up."

The wood was warm to the touch, vibrating with a faint, dormant pulse that made my fingertips tingle. "So... what now?"

Chaos sheathed his blade, his gaze locking onto the distant, hazy horizon. "We track down the rest of those energy signatures."

The wind rushed through the canyon, filling the space between us. I ran my thumb over the staff's intricate, eroded carvings. "What do you think is actually out there?"

He looked back at me, his expression deadpan. "Probably something incredibly important."

I shoved his shoulder. "You can never be serious for more than two minutes."

He laughed, though the sound was tired. "Fine. It could be a complete waste of time. Fifty-fifty."

I pulled my knees to my chest. "I just want answers," I whispered, the weight of our lost home pressing down on me again.

Chaos's demeanor shifted. He knelt beside me, his calloused hand brushing the dirt from my cheek. "We will," he said, the arrogant edge completely gone from his voice. "We'll find them."

I leaned into his palm, grounding myself in the rough, familiar texture of his skin.

The sky above us began to bleed into deep violet and bruised orange as the massive sun dipped below the canopy. The sharp scent of incoming rain cut through the lingering dust. I closed my eyes, letting the cool wind wash over my face. His humor, his cockiness—it was his armor. A way to anchor us both when the universe felt too vast.

"Thank you," I breathed.

His fingers gripped my shoulder, solid and unyielding. "Together."

"Together," I echoed, forcing a tired smile.

We pushed ourselves up from the dirt, turning our backs on the chasm as the first heavy drops of rain began to fall.

"So," Chaos mused, his boots crunching against the gravel as we headed back toward the Arkenon, "do you think we could teach one of those giant lizards to talk? Might speed up the recon."

A genuine laugh escaped my chest, breaking the heavy tension. The terrain ahead was dark, hostile, and unknown, but as long as he was walking beside me, the weight of the universe felt a little lighter.

Chapter 3: Terrors of the Past

Ash drifted down from the choked sky like grey snow, coating the skeletal remains of Talon.

I stood alone in the wasteland. This was supposed to be our new beginning. The massive, curved bulkheads of the frigate that brought our ancestors here jutted out of the scorched earth like the ribs of a rotting leviathan. They had stripped the ship piece by piece to build a sanctuary, only to turn it into a tomb.

Where lush, engineered vegetation once grew, deep craters now bled noxious, yellow fumes into the heavy air. The wind tasted sharply of iron and scorched synthetics. The unmistakable scent of a massacre.

My boots crunched over shattered glass and blackened earth as I wandered through the ruins. At the edge of a collapsed trench, my boot clipped something half-buried in the ash. I knelt, my trembling fingers brushing the soot away. It was a plasteel toy—a child's model of a starship, warped and melted down to the core from intense heat.

My throat seized. The silence of the wasteland shattered, instantly replaced by a deafening auditory assault.

Flashes of warped, desperate faces.

Hands clawing at airlock doors.

The high-pitched whine of plasma fire tearing through residential habs.

The screams of our own crew, drowning out the pleading of those who just wanted to leave.

We had traveled across the stars to escape the hunger for power, but we had just packed the disease in our cargo hold. We had brought the very worst of our ancestral world and planted it in fresh soil.

"You can't build a future on rot, Gaia."

The voice cut through the overlapping screams. Chaos stepped out from the thick, acrid smoke behind me. In the dream, he wasn't carrying the weariness of our journey. He looked exactly as he had on the day Talon fell—eyes dark, armor scarred. He stepped closer, his hand landing heavy and solid on my shoulder.

I didn't look away from the melted toy in my palm. "They were our people, Chaos. Our crew. We were supposed to be the new beginning, and we failed them."

Chaos stepped around me, forcing me to meet his gaze. The smoke curled around his boots. "They failed us," he said, his voice a low, vibrating rumble. "Theia was the objective. The original plan. They let fear make their choices. They chose the false comfort of a dead rock over the uncertainty of the stars."

He reached out, his thumb catching a warm tear as it tracked through the ash on my cheek. "We carry the memory of what we were supposed to be. We have to keep fighting for that."

He cupped his armored hands over mine, pressing the melted toy between our palms. "They were terrified of the unknown, Gaia. The choice between comfort and survival tore them apart."

My fingers tightened around the ruined plasteel. "What if Theia is just a ghost?" I whispered to the ash. "What if we are truly the last ones?"

My eyes snapped open.

A violent gasp tore through my lungs. I bolted upright, my fingers clawing not at ash, but at the cold, unforgiving deck plating of the Arkenon.

My heart hammered against my ribs like a trapped bird. Cold sweat dripped down the back of my neck, chilling me in the humid air bleeding through the ship's vents. Pale, fractured moonlight filtered through the observation window, casting long shadows across the cargo bay. I forced my breathing to slow, desperate to sever the scent of blood in my dream from the damp, earthy smell of the reptilian world outside.

Beside me, the shadows shifted. Chaos didn't just wake up; he snapped into consciousness, his hand instinctively reaching for the empty space where his sword usually rested before his eyes adjusted to the moonlight.

He looked at me, his chest rising and falling heavily. The hard, warrior edge in his eyes melted away, leaving only a bone-deep exhaustion. "The night terrors?" his voice was a gravelly, sleep-rough whisper.

I pulled my knees to my chest, nodding. My voice was completely raw. "The same one. Talon. The betrayal... it just feels so real."

Chaos abandoned his bedroll, sliding across the metal floor until he was sitting flush against me. "It was real, Gaia. Unfortunately."

He didn't offer empty platitudes or arrogant jokes. He simply wrapped his arms around me, pulling me into the solid, grounding heat of his chest. I buried my face in his shoulder, gripping the fabric of his shirt as the lingering terror of the nightmare finally broke, giving way to silent, shaking tears.

Chapter 4: The Guardians Call

The Arkenon skimmed the dense, emerald canopy, our thrusters kicking up a wake of displaced leaves. I leaned against the observation deck railing, the heavy, humid air sticking to my skin.

"From the stories the elders told," I murmured, watching a flock of leathery-winged creatures scatter from our flight path, "I pictured this place... differently."

Chaos stood beside me, his eyes locked on the sprawling green horizon. "It's vicious," he admitted, his voice barely rising over the wind. "But it has its own brutal beauty."

The moment shattered. A roar, so deep it vibrated the metal deck plating beneath my boots, erupted from the foliage directly ahead. The canopy violently parted. A massive theropod lunged upward, its reptilian eyes dead-locked on the Arkenon.

"I don't think we're welcome," Chaos muttered, his hand already a blur as it found the hilt of his sword.

My own energy crackled to life, raising the hair on my arms. I thrust my hand forward, sending a pressurized kinetic blast directly at the beast's chest. The impact sounded like a thunderclap, but the creature barely flinched, using its sheer momentum to absorb the blow.

"Looks like we have to do this the hard way," Chaos grinned, unsheathing his blade.

The beast roared again, its massive, razor-lined jaws snapping shut with a sickening crunch just inches from the ship's port hull.

I didn't think; I just reacted. I gripped the weathered staff we had claimed at the chasm and thrust it downward.

It didn't just glow. The wood thrummed violently in my hands, channeling a surge of violet, ionized energy that instantly tethered to the theropod. The beast shrieked, a terrifying, guttural sound that quickly morphed into a panicked whimper. Its massive body convulsed in mid-air. I twisted the staff, grinding my teeth against the physical resistance of the tether, and forced the energy downward. The unseen kinetic weight slammed the apex predator into the dirt, pinning it like an insect. Its powerful limbs trembled, completely paralyzed by the overwhelming force.

I held it there for three seconds, feeling the terrifying, raw authority of the staff coursing through my veins, before snapping my wrist back to sever the connection.

The beast collapsed into the undergrowth with a thunderous thud. As the violet glow faded from the wood, an eerie, breathless silence fell over the jungle.

I turned to Chaos. His sword was still drawn, his eyes wide as he stared at the spot where the monster had fallen, then down to the stick in my hand.

"What just happened?" he asked, the adrenaline making his voice tight.

I looked at the eroded, ancient wood. It felt impossibly heavy now. "I don't know," I breathed. "But this is far more than a walking stick."

The Arkenon's proximity alarm chimed, pulling us back to reality. The telemetry array flashed red, indicating the energy signal was directly below us. Chaos took the helm, dropping the ship into a tight, muddy clearing surrounded by towering ferns.

He grabbed a handheld tracking terminal, and we descended the ramp into the suffocating heat.

The jungle was a sensory assault. The air was a thick soup of decaying vegetation and wet earth. A cacophony of shrieks, clicks, and rustling branches echoed from every direction. I kept my back close to Chaos's, my eyes darting toward every shadow that melted between the trees. We were being watched. I could feel it in the back of my neck.

The tracker led us through the thicket until the organic chaos gave way to geometric order.

Ancient, crumbling stone walls choked by thick vines emerged from the shadows. Moss-covered statues, their faces eroded by time and rain, lined a broken path. The architecture didn't look natural; it looked like a scar of civilization swallowed by the wild. We followed the path to the gaping maw of a languishing temple.

Chaos tapped the handheld screen. It flickered, then flatlined.

He looked up, meeting my eyes. "Signal is dead. But we've come this far."

"Agreed," I said, stepping into the damp, shadowed archway.

The temple felt less like a sanctuary and more like a subterranean excavation. We navigated the labyrinthine corridors by the pale glow of my energy, the air growing stale and thick with the scent of undisturbed dust.

As we descended into an expansive, branching chamber, a low, wet growl echoed off the stone walls.

I froze, shifting my weight into a battle stance. The growl deepened into a guttural, bone-rattling snarl. From the pitch-black mouth of the corridor ahead, a hulking silhouette detached itself from the shadows. It moved like a wingless dragon, scales scraping against stone.

Chaos stepped forward, lowering the tip of his sword. "Easy now," he commanded, his voice a dangerous, warning rumble. "We aren't looking for trouble."

He threw a smirk over his shoulder at me. "See? I can do it your way."

"You think it understands a word you're saying?" I shot back, keeping my eyes on the beast.

"It'll understand the tone."

But as the creature stalked into the dim light, its slitted eyes narrowing, I felt a distinct shift in the air. This wasn't the feral, mindless aggression of the theropod. Its predatory stance was calculated. Intelligent.

"Chaos," I warned, watching its muscles coil. "It's striking!"

The guardian lunged.

Chaos didn't flinch. He pivoted, his sword flashing in a deadly, silver arc. The blade met the beast's scaled hide with a deafening screech of metal. The guardian roared in agony, staggering backward, its golden eyes burning with fury.

Before it could recover, I slammed the base of the staff into the stone floor. A concussive flash of kinetic light erupted, blinding the creature. Chaos moved like a blur, exploiting the stun to press the offensive. The guardian fought with savage, desperate ferocity, its claws carving gouges into the stone walls, but it couldn't match our synchronized rhythm.

With a final, echoing roar, the beast collapsed. Dark blood pooled on the ancient stone.

My chest heaved as I leaned against my staff, the adrenaline slowly bleeding out of my system. Chaos wiped his blade, his jaw set in a hard line. We had killed to survive before, but this felt wrong. It didn't feel like a hunt; it felt like we had just broken through a lock.

"Intruders."

The hiss slithered through the chamber, echoing off the high ceilings. "You dare defile this sacred ground?"

We spun, weapons raised, searching the suffocating shadows.

A reptilian humanoid stepped into the pale light. He stood upright, draped in tattered, ceremonial garments. A long, forked tongue flicked past his scaled lips, tasting the copper in the air.

"This area is forbidden," he hissed, his golden eyes darting from the slain guardian to us. "Turn back, or face the consequences."

Chaos didn't lower his sword. "We mean no harm. We only seek answers."

"Answers?" The creature let out a sharp, clicking laugh. "What answers could you possibly find in this forsaken place?"

I stepped past Chaos, lowering my staff. "The truth about our ancestral world. Our ship tracked a massive Theian energy signature to this exact spot."

The reptilian's eyes widened, the hostility momentarily eclipsed by shock. "Your ancestral world? What makes you arrogant enough to claim this place belongs to you?"

"We thought this was a Theian temple," Chaos answered, his tone flat.

The creature drew himself up, standing taller. "The paths and archways you walked to get here were carved by my people. I am Kameel. My nation has protected these grounds for millennia."

"Protected what, exactly?" Chaos challenged. "Because our instruments say whatever is down here is connected to our home."

I held up a hand, silencing Chaos before he could escalate the tension. Taking a slow breath, I explained everything. The fall of our colony. The coordinates in the data logs. Our desperate, fragile hope that this violent, overgrown planet was the cradle of our civilization.

Kameel stood as still as a statue, his golden eyes burning into mine, searching for deception. Finally, his rigid posture softened.

"Your story is steeped in tragedy," he hissed softly. "But the air around you does not taste of lies."

I let out a breath I hadn't realized I was holding. Chaos finally lowered his blade.

"Thank you," I said.

Kameel turned toward the dark archway behind him. "Follow. There is something you must see."

My pulse quickened as we trailed the reptilian guide deeper into the earth. The atmosphere shifted drastically. The stale air was replaced by a strange, static hum that made the hair on my arms stand up. The rough stone walls transitioned into a smooth, seamless metallic surface that pulsed with a faint, internal luminescence.

"These walls," Kameel said, tracing a scaled finger over the smooth surface, "are made of a material beyond our comprehension. It cannot be broken, forged, or replicated."

We stepped into a vast, glowing inner sanctum. In the center sat a monolithic altar, covered in deep, precise etchings.

"The writing was already here when my ancestors discovered it," Kameel continued, reverently bowing his head. "We could not carve into it if we tried."

Chaos stepped up to the wall. He stared at the seamless metal, his brow furrowing. Without a word, he reversed his grip on his sword and drove the tip of his blade hard into the wall, dragging it downward.

Sparks showered the floor. A high-pitched screech echoed through the room, leaving a thin, distinct silver scratch in the pristine surface.

Kameel gasped, taking a stumbling step backward.

"Plasmetal," Chaos whispered, staring at his blade. "Forged from star plasma. The only thing in the universe dense enough to cut it..."

"...is itself," I finished, staring at the scratch.

Kameel looked at us as if we were gods made flesh. "You... you mark the unmarkable stone. It is proof." He rushed to the altar, pointing a trembling claw at the central inscription. "The prophecies! They state that the Descendants will return here for redemption!"

"What else do the stories say?" Chaos demanded, stepping closer to the altar.

"You cannot read them?" Kameel asked, confused.

Chaos scanned the symbols. "No. It's not our language. Maybe a dead dialect."

"How do you know what it says?" I asked Kameel.

"I cannot read it either," he admitted, his voice dropping to a hushed whisper.

"The translations were passed down orally for a hundred generations. Taught to us by the ones who first tasked us with protecting this sanctum. Visitors from another world. The Ancients."

Before I could process the sheer magnitude of what he was saying, the floor violently dropped beneath our feet.

A localized tremor hit with the force of an explosive impact. The plasmetal walls groaned under immense pressure, and a cascade of dust and debris rained down from the dark ceiling above.

Chapter 5: Voice of Tartarus

The tremor didn't fade. It deepened into a localized, mechanical hum that vibrated the fillings in my teeth.

The ancient symbols carved into the altar ignited. A blinding, searing orange light flooded the sanctum. The solid, seamless plasmetal wall in front of us didn't slide open; it dissolved. The metal fractured into floating geometric shards, silently rearranging themselves to reveal a perfectly arched corridor.

A gust of air rushed out of the dark. It wasn't the damp, decaying scent of the jungle. It was freezing, sterile, and metallic—the preserved breath of a dead world.

Chaos immediately shifted his weight, putting his body between me and the dark passage, his sword raised to strike.

Kameel's golden eyes dilated into thin slits. He backed slowly toward the entrance. "That... has never happened before," he hissed, his claws scraping nervously against the stone.

"Stay here," I told him, gripping my staff tight enough that my knuckles ached.

Chaos and I stepped through the breach. The moment my boot crossed the threshold, a beam of hard, white light snapped down from the ceiling. Particles of dust ignited in the air as a massive, translucent figure constructed itself, layer by layer, in the center of the hidden chamber. It stood ten feet tall, clad in armor that mirrored Chaos's, but rendered in fractured, flickering light.

"Greetings, Theians, and local ally," the figure boomed. The voice didn't come from a speaker; it resonated directly inside my skull. "I am Theia's Advanced Real-time Tactical and Response Universal System. T.A.R.T.A.R.U.S. I have waited a very long time for your arrival."

I stared at the towering projection, my heart hammering against my ribs. "You said Theian." My voice was quiet, trembling despite my efforts to control it. "We've been searching for our home. The coordinates led us here, but this planet is too wild. Too dense. Is this... is this Theia?"

The hologram flickered with a burst of static. "Yes. And no. You are standing on a corpse stitched to a stranger."

Chaos lowered his blade an inch. "Two worlds combined?"

"A cosmic waltz," Tartarus replied. "Two planets dancing around their star. Their tempo was misaligned by a fraction of a degree. One crashed into the other, merging their masses. But this cataclysm occurred long after the Great Darkness fell upon our people."

"Great Darkness?" I echoed.

"Observe."

Tartarus didn't just project an image; he overwrote the room. The sterile metal walls vanished. Suddenly, I was standing under a brilliant, perfectly blue sky. The air smelled of clean ozone and blooming flora. Towering, elegant spires of glass and plasmetal stretched into the clouds. Theians walked the streets around me, their faces bright and unburdened.

"This was Theia at its apex," Tartarus's voice boomed from the sky itself. "A world of absolute prosperity."

I reached out, my fingers brushing against the phantom projection of a smiling child running past. My chest ached with a sudden, violent grief. This was what we had lost.

But the air abruptly turned freezing cold. The blue sky bled into an oppressive, bruised crimson. The joyful chatter distorted into screams and the deafening whine of plasma fire. The elegant spires around me began to crumble, raining holographic glass down on us. I flinched, throwing my arms up, but the debris phased right through me.

Through the smoke, I saw Theians turning on each other, their faces contorted with rage and desperation.

"A malevolent sorceress named Ayin injected a virus into the hearts of our people," Tartarus explained, his voice dipping into a sorrowful drone. "She whispered insidious lies from the shadows. She didn't need an army. She weaponized our own envy. The civilization ripped itself apart long before the planetary collision."

The red sky dissolved. The screams faded into silence. We were back in the freezing, hidden chamber.

"The collision ended two worlds," Tartarus said, the white light of his projection dimming slightly. "But when the dust settled, this new world was born. Genesis."

"Genesis," I whispered, letting the word roll off my tongue. The weight of it felt right.

"There are two concentrated masses of Theian wreckage on Genesis," Tartarus commanded. "The collision buried them. They were stocked as emergency armories before the fall. The architects knew weapons would be useless against Ayin's mind-games in a massive population. But they calculated that if a small, uncorrupted strike force ever returned, they would need overwhelming firepower."

Chaos stepped closer to the hologram, his jaw tight. "You're saying this sorceress survived the planet cracking in half?"

Tartarus's eyes shifted, locking onto Chaos. "She orchestrated the downfall of a species. She slumbers deep within the core of Genesis. But your arrival will trigger her awakening. Once she senses you, she will rise to finish what she started."

The towering hologram extended an open palm toward us. "You carry the raw potential of the Ancients in your blood. But without the armory, you will burn."

A sudden, sharp beam of white light shot from Tartarus’s hand directly into the tracking terminal holstered at Chaos's hip.

The device hissed, emitting a puff of smoke. Chaos ripped it off his belt as the cracked screen violently rebooted, rendering a flawless, three-dimensional topographic map of Genesis, marked with a single, pulsing gold coordinate.

"I have synchronized the network," Tartarus said, his form beginning to dissolve back into dust particles. "Seek the armory. And remember... the future has yet to be written."

The light snapped off, plunging the room back into heavy shadows.

"Actually, it has!"

I jumped, turning back toward the archway. Kameel was leaning against the plasmetal frame, casually picking at his teeth with a claw.

I gave him a bewildered look. "Do you know something we don't?"

"Nah," Kameel shrugged, his forked tongue flicking the air. "It just felt like a really dramatic thing to say after a ghost finishes talking."

Chaos let out a sharp exhale, shaking his head.

"I must inform my tribe of this," Kameel continued, his tone shifting to something far more serious. "If there is a slumbering evil waking up, we will fight to protect our home and these sacred grounds. I can assemble a hunting party to accompany you to these coordinates."

Chaos holstered the sparking datapad. "Don't. Just warn your people to brace themselves. If we run into this sorceress, a hunting party will just be collateral damage."

Chapter 6: Divine Armor

The Arkenon tore through the dense cloud layer, our thrusters screaming in protest against the heavy atmosphere. I couldn't blink away the phantom sting of plasma fire or the scent of burning plasmetal from Tartarus's projection. The vibrant streets of our ancestors, the joyous faces—all of it shattered, poisoned by a single entity.

My knuckles turned white where I gripped the ancient staff. The wood thrummed against my palms, a steady, pulsing heartbeat that grounded me against the violent shaking of the hull.

Chaos sat at the helm, his jaw set so tight a muscle ticked in his cheek. "She'll pay for it," he said, his voice a low, lethal rumble over the roar of the engines.

"She will," I echoed, staring out the viewport. "Whatever it takes."

Chaos tapped the cracked, smoking glass of his datapad. "We're right on top of the coordinates. The energy spike here matches the mass buried in the crust."

"It makes sense," I murmured, watching the sprawling horizon of green and brown blur beneath us. "Let's see what the architects left us to fight a god."

As we initiated the descent, the sky didn't just darken; it bruised. The clouds thickened into an unnatural, heavy canopy that suffocated the sunlight. Static electricity danced across the viewport glass, making the hair on my arms stand on end. The air pressure plummeted in an instant, popping my ears.

"The atmosphere is shifting," I warned, gripping the console.

"I feel it," Chaos replied, his eyes narrowing as he guided the ship down. "Weapons hot the second the ramp drops."

The Arkenon's landing gear sank into the mud of a massive, shadowed clearing.

The moment the hatch hissed open, a wave of thick, humid air washed over us. It didn't smell like the rotting vegetation of the jungle; it tasted sharply of oxidized copper and ozone. There were no shrieks of raptors, no snapping of branches. The entire ecosystem was paralyzed by an unnerving, absolute silence.

We stepped into the mud, our backs to each other, sweeping the perimeter. The coordinates led us toward a jagged grotto, swallowed by hanging vines. We pushed through the dense brush until the organic chaos abruptly gave way to a smooth, seamless plasmetal corridor plunging straight into the earth.

"It feels Theian," I whispered, the ambient static making my skin prickle.

"Yeah," Chaos agreed, his thumb resting on the pommel of his sword. "And it doesn't feel empty."

At the end of the corridor, massive plasmetal doors blocked our path. Glowing, intricate runes were etched deep into the surface. As I focused on them, my vision blurred for a fraction of a second. A sharp ping echoed in my skull as the network sync Tartarus had forced into our tech translated the dead dialect directly into my mind.

Generator.

Safety Equipment Required.

"What do you think that means?" I asked, tracing the glowing translation.

"I don't know," Chaos smirked, patting the hilt of his blade. "But I brought my safety equipment."

A sub-harmonic hum resonated from the floorboards. The ground trembled as the colossal doors dissolved, the metal sliding seamlessly into the walls.

A blast of cold, sterile air rushed out to greet us. Glowing crystalline veins pulsed along the high, vaulted ceilings, casting a pale blue light over a massive armory. The chamber was lined with weapons and gear completely foreign to the primitive ruins we had seen so far.

Chaos immediately gravitated toward a rack of sleek, perfectly balanced blades. He lifted a sword, his thumb instinctively finding a twisting mechanism built into the grip. With a sharp twist, the core of the weapon ignited. The edge of the blade shimmered, bleeding raw, condensed starlight into the dim room. Without a second thought, he discarded his old sword, tossing it onto the floor.

I didn't care about the blades. My eyes were drawn to the back of the vault.

It wasn't the dull, utilitarian scrap we were used to surviving in. The armor displayed before me radiated a faint, inner luminescence, like liquid gold frozen into overlapping, intricate scales.

I reached out, lifting a gauntlet. It weighed almost nothing. As I slid my hand inside, the metal didn't just strap on—it contracted. The golden scales shifted and locked, seamlessly sealing over my skin with a warm, empowering hum that synced perfectly with my pulse.

"Chaos, look at this," I breathed, turning my hands over, watching the golden metal flex without the slightest restriction to my joints.

He stepped up beside me, the starlight from his new blade reflecting in his wide eyes. "It's not just armor. It's a masterpiece."

We stripped off our travel-worn gear. Chaos locked a set of golden greaves over his shins and knees, the intricate, sweeping designs accentuating the powerful muscles in his legs. I fastened a sleek breastplate over my chest, the metal conforming to my shape like a second skin. I strapped the sheath Chaos had given me just above my right ankle, snapping it perfectly into place over the golden weave.

We didn't look like scavengers anymore. As I rolled my shoulders, testing the absolute freedom of movement, a wave of overwhelming confidence washed the exhaustion from my bones. We looked like the vengeance of a fallen world.

As I turned, a strange resonance tugged at my chest. Mounted on the far wall was a specialized harness bracket featuring two deep indentations. One was shaped like a massive trident. The other perfectly mirrored the gnarled, weathered contours of the staff currently gripped in my right hand.

I stepped closer, aligning the wood with the slot. It hovered for a split second before magnetically snapping into place with a heavy *clack*. I pulled the multi-slotted holster from the wall and strapped it across my back, securing the staff perfectly over my shoulder.

"Now that you are properly armed," a voice boomed from the walls, vibrating the floorboards. "It is time for the next phase of your preparation."

Before I could ask what Tartarus meant, the armory dissolved.

The weapon racks, the glowing crystals, the plasmetal walls—all of it fractured into light and sank into the floor. The space expanded outward, stretching into a massive, grid-lined arena. The air grew thick as distorted, hard-light silhouettes materialized around us, taking the shapes of massive beasts and armed combatants.

"This is where you will master your new arsenal," Tartarus explained from the ether. "You must be ready for the sorceress."

Chaos grinned, dropping into a fighting stance, his starlight blade humming. "Sounds like fun."

My lungs burned. My knuckles bruised against hard-light projections. Time lost its meaning inside the arena.

The next hours—or days—were a blur of kinetic violence. Chaos and I didn't just practice; we bled, pushed to the absolute brink by the relentless holographic onslaught. Tartarus's voice corrected our posture, guiding our strikes from the shadows.

I learned to channel the kinetic shockwaves not just through the staff, but directly through the golden gauntlets, shattering solid-light constructs with the raw force of my fists. Chaos became a tempest of light, his new blade slicing through obstacles with terrifying, lethal fluidity.

The esoteric teachings of the Ancients began to make sense in my muscles rather than my mind. We stopped tripping over each other's footwork. We moved as one cohesive, synchronized unit, our golden armor flashing as we dismantled every simulation Tartarus threw at us.

Finally, the hard-light projections shattered into pixelated dust and did not reform.

"You adapt well," Tartarus declared, the arena dissolving back into the cold, quiet vault of the armory. "You are no longer mere survivors. But to defeat Ayin, you will need armies. Two nations inhabit Genesis: the Repterians and the Aquarians. Seek their assistance."

A notification pinged in my helmet display. "I have marked the location of the

Aquarians on your map," Tartarus concluded. "Go forth. Fulfill your destiny."

"We won't let you down," Chaos swore, his chest heaving as he sheathed his starlight blade.

When we stepped back out of the grotto and into the mud, the oppressive, suffocating silence of the jungle had shattered. The screeching of raptors and the rustling of heavy foliage filled the air. Small, winged critters darted between the ferns. It was as if activating the armory had lifted a heavy, toxic blanket off the ecosystem.

"We're already making a difference," I smiled, letting the warm, humid air hit my face.

We boarded the Arkenon, our boots echoing heavily on the metal ramp. Chaos initiated the launch sequence, his golden greaves gleaming under the console lights.

"The Aquarians are at the second energy source," he said, the thrusters whining as we broke through the dense canopy and shot into the bruised sky.

I looked out at the endless, sprawling horizon. The fear that had plagued my nightmares was gone, replaced by the steady, humming power of the golden gauntlets on my hands.

"Take us to the Aquarians."

Chapter 7: Scars of Yesterday

The warm, artificial light of the colony star faded into the harsh, strobing red of emergency sirens.

I wasn't on the Arkenon. I was back in the colony’s central plaza, the air thick with the smell of sweat and oxidized metal. The memory refused to stay buried. It always played out behind my eyelids with the same suffocating clarity.

Captain Delza stood on the raised platform, his fist slamming onto the podium. "We are scavengers here!" his voice boomed over the restless, surging crowd. "Theia is our birthright! We must return to the roots of our ancestors!"

Dr. Rioma stepped into the light beside him. He didn't shout. He raised his hands, his voice smooth and carrying like oiled glass over the PA system. "Theia is a graveyard. We have soil here. We have atmospheric processors. We can build a culture free from the ghosts of the past. A true new beginning."

The visions clashed, the tension in the plaza pulling tight enough to snap. I could feel the static in the air. The murmurs of the crowd escalated into shouting. Shouting fractured into shoving.

Then came the flash.

The violence erupted like a localized supernova. The deafening screech of plasma fire tore through the residential hab-blocks, turning the air to ozone and burning meat. I tasted copper as an elbow caught my jaw in the crushing panic of the mob. Friends turned on neighbors, their faces contorted into masks of feral survival.

Through the thick, choking black smoke, a hand grabbed my wrist.

Chaos. His dark eyes were wide, reflecting the burning infrastructure around us. His jaw was slack with a horror that mirrored my own. We didn't speak. We ran. We sprinted blindly through the maintenance corridors, not looking back at the bodies trampling each other, until we breached the outer hangars and found the Arkenon waiting in the shadows.

The nightmare shifted to the observation deck. As the thrusters engaged,

I looked down through the viewport. Our colony, our unified sanctuary, burned. The flames painted the heavy clouds in bruised purples and sickening, arterial reds. My stomach violently heaved, battery acid burning the back of my throat—

"Night terror?"

The smoke vanished. My eyes snapped open.

I was lying on the cold deck of the Arkenon, my chest heaving. The dim, blue lights of the navigation console washed over the cargo bay. My fingers were locked in a death grip around the edges of my new golden breastplate.

Chaos was kneeling beside me. He wasn't in his old, ash-stained gear; the intricate golden greaves caught the pale light of the cabin. He reached out, his calloused thumb rough against my cheek as he wiped away cold moisture I hadn't realized was there.

"The same one," I rasped, my throat feeling like sandpaper. "The plaza. The screaming. It just gets more vivid every time I close my eyes."

He didn't offer empty platitudes. The metal of his armor clinked softly as he shifted his weight, wrapping a heavy, grounding arm around my shoulders. "We're here," he rumbled, the deep vibration in his chest steadying my frantic pulse. "We're alive. And we are going to build a life on this rock that puts our ancestors to shame."

His words anchored me, pulling me back from the edge of the abyss. I leaned into the cool gold of his armor, letting his steady breathing sync with my own. "I know," I whispered.

We sat on the deck in silence for a long moment. The Arkenon hummed smoothly around us, a metal sanctuary tearing through the night sky.

I looked up toward the viewport. Outside, the bruised darkness of Genesis was cracking open. The first harsh, white light of dawn bled across the endless, sprawling ocean below us. A new day.

I pushed myself up. The servos in my golden gauntlets whined softly, the weight of the armor filling me with a heavy, thrumming power. The nausea was gone, replaced by a hardening resolve. I walked to the helm, looking down at the topographic map Tartarus had burned into our console.

"Today is a new day," I said, my voice losing its tremor as I locked onto the pulsing coordinates in the middle of the sea. "We have Aquarians to find."

Chaos stood up beside me, the dawn light catching the hilt of his starlight blade. The shadows of the nightmare retreated, burned away by the rising sun.

Chapter 8: The Serpent's Wake

The Arkenon tore across the sky, leaving a wake of turbulent air over the endless, churning expanse of the Genesis ocean.

I stood at the observation deck railing, the howling wind whipping my crimson braid against the newly forged golden breastplate. The metal hummed, a steady vibration that pushed back against the biting chill of the sea spray. Below us, the water was a deep, bruising navy, hiding the second Theian energy signature miles beneath the crushing depths.

"What do you think is actually down there?" I shouted over the roar of the thrusters.

Chaos stood at the helm, his starlight blade securely strapped to his hip. He didn't look up from the navigation console. "Hopefully, the rest of our arsenal."

The telemetry array blared a sudden, piercing klaxon.

Before Chaos could touch the controls, the ocean below us erupted. A geyser of white foam exploded upward, and the sky darkened. A colossal silhouette breached the surface, its sheer mass dwarfing the Arkenon. Thick, stone scales the size of our hull plates sloughed off thousands of gallons of seawater. Two eyes, burning with the malevolent, hyper-focused red glare of an apex predator, locked onto us.

My stomach bottomed out. The air pressure dropped so fast my ears popped.

"Evasive!" I screamed, lunging for the co-pilot seat and slamming the restraints over my armor.

Chaos yanked the yoke hard right. The Arkenon banked violently. G-force pinned me to the seat as the creature lunged. A deafening, metallic shriek tore through the cabin as razor-sharp teeth scraped the starboard hull, ripping away a layer of armor plating before the massive jaws snapped shut on empty air.

The beast didn't fall back into the sea. It contorted its massive, serpentine body, defying gravity to match our ascent. Every twisting dive Chaos executed, the serpent mirrored, its massive jaws snapping inches from our rear thrusters.

I unholstered my staff, the ancient wood instantly vibrating to life in my hands, radiating a defensive violet aura. "We can't outrun it!"

"It owns the water!" Chaos yelled, his hands flying across the terminal to reroute power to the engines. "We have to drag it back to land!"

A catastrophic jolt rattled my teeth. The cabin lights flickered and died, instantly replaced by the strobe of red emergency flares. The serpent's jaws had clamped down on the tail thrusters.

Gravity inverted. The nose of the Arkenon pitched straight down.

"Brace!" Chaos roared over the screaming metal.

The impact was a wall of concrete. The viewport instantly shattered. Freezing, high-pressure brine slammed into the cockpit, violently tearing me from my seat. The cold was an absolute shock, freezing the air in my lungs. The Arkenon was sinking like a stone, the dark water swallowing us instantly.

I kicked frantically, fighting the disorientation. My golden gauntlets gripped the edge of the shattered viewport, and I pulled myself through the twisted metal. The ocean pressure immediately crushed against my chest. My lungs burned, demanding oxygen I didn't have.

I turned back to see Chaos pulling himself free, his golden greaves kicking through the debris.

Above us, the faint, shimmering light from the surface was eclipsed. The serpent circled, its massive coils creating a whirlpool that dragged at our limbs. The burning red eyes zeroed in on us, cutting through the pitch-black water.

It dove.

I raised my staff, bracing to unleash a kinetic shockwave, knowing it wouldn't be enough against the crushing pressure of the depths.

A searing beam of blue light cut through the dark from the abyss below us.

It struck the serpent directly under its jaw. The beast recoiled, releasing a cascade of pressurized bubbles as it roared in pain. Its red eyes darted toward the source of the light before it whipped its tail and retreated into the inky black.

My vision began to blur. The lack of oxygen was turning the edges of my sight dark.

Shadows moved in the water below us. Slender figures propelled themselves upward with impossible speed. As they closed the distance, the faint blue glow from their weapons illuminated pale skin, webbed fingers, and gills flaring along the sides of their necks. Their weapons—sleek, glowing tridents—pulsed with the exact same frequency as my staff.

Two of them grabbed my arms. I didn't have the strength to fight. They pulled us downward, their momentum tearing us through the water faster than any predator.

The crushing black gave way to an explosion of bioluminescence. A sprawling metropolis of bright, neon-glowing coral rested inside a massive, transparent dome. They dragged us beneath the city's platform and up through a circular moon pool.

We broke the surface.

I collapsed onto the hard, smooth floor of the airlock, coughing up bitter brine. The air here was crisp, cool, and mechanically cycled. Above me, several more of the pale figures stood with tridents lowered.

I rolled onto my back, my chest heaving as my lungs greedily took in the oxygen. Beside me, Chaos pushed himself up onto one knee, coughing violently. The golden armor clung to us, shedding water perfectly.

"Thank you," I gasped, my throat raw.

One of the figures stepped forward, lowering her trident. "The pleasure is ours," she said, her voice carrying a strange, melodic resonance. "Our council humbly requests your presence."

The airlock cycled, leading us directly into the heart of the metropolis. The architecture was organic, grown rather than built, humming with a warm, bioluminescent energy.

They escorted us to the center of the city, into a massive structure shaped like a spiraling sundial. Inside, a group of elders sat upon thrones carved from polished, iridescent shells. In the center sat an elder woman, her flowing white hair shifting as if still caught in a current.

"Welcome to Siren's Hollow. I am Thalassa, Chief of the Aquarian Council," she spoke, the acoustics of the shell projecting her voice perfectly. "We only know of the Repterians on the surface. What world do you claim? And what brings you to our depths?"

I stepped forward, the water evaporating off my skin. I didn't waste time on pleasantries. I told her everything. The fall of our colony, the truth of Genesis, the armory, and the warning from Tartarus.

When I spoke the name Ayin, the temperature in the room seemed to drop. The council members shifted uncomfortably, the gills on their necks flaring.

Thalassa leaned forward, her wise eyes locking onto mine. "That name is not unknown to the depths. Legends speak of a great darkness that poisoned the surface world long ago. A myth. A cautionary tale."

"It's not a myth," Chaos said, his voice hard, his hand resting on the hilt of his sword. "And she is waking up."

Thalassa nodded slowly, her expression grim. "We have sensed a growing unrest in the deep trenches. A stirring of shadows we shamefully dismissed as geothermal activity. If the sorceress returns, the oceans will boil alongside the surface."

"That is why we need your archives," I said, stepping closer to the throne. "Tartarus told us there are weapons hidden on Genesis. If there is a way to stop her, your people might have the key."

Thalassa stood. "We have guarded the secrets beneath the waves for millennia. Prepare the ancient archives," she commanded the guards at the door. She looked down at us. "You are granted full access."

Hours bled into a timeless haze inside the colossal, submerged archive chamber. Floating alongside Aquarian scholars, we scoured through massive, waterproof scripts and etched stone tablets. Dust from the ancient stones clouded the water inside the pressurized archive bubble. My eyes ached, and frustration was beginning to set in.

"Here!" a scholar suddenly gasped, pointing a webbed finger at a faded, glowing inscription on a basalt slab. "A weapon capable of banishing darkness. The Tidal Trident. Forged from a dying star and blessed by a Guardian of Divinity."

A Guardian of Divinity. The childhood myths of cosmic entities holding the universe together flashed through my mind.

Chaos stepped up to the slab. "Where is it?"

The scholar's pale face lost even more color. "The Abyssal Trench. Protected by a guardian of tremendous rage."

A cold shiver raced up my spine, settling in the base of my neck. "We don't have a choice," I stated, staring at the translation.

Thalassa, hovering near the entrance, nodded. "Lochlan will guide you. He knows the Trench better than any Aquarian alive. But be warned. The darkness down there changes things."

We were outfitted immediately. Over our golden armor, the Aquarians sealed us into sleek, high-tech sub-dermal suits. The material felt like a second skin, actively regulating our body temperature and neutralizing drag. They strapped compact, mechanical rebreathers over our faces. The masks bit securely into the skin along our jawlines, emitting a soft hiss as they extracted oxygen directly from the water.

We followed Lochlan, a silent, heavily scarred Aquarian, out of a specialized pressure lock at the base of the city.

The descent was immediate and terrifying. The bioluminescence of Siren's Hollow faded into a pinprick of light above us, then vanished completely. The pressure against the golden breastplate increased exponentially, a physical weight trying to crush my ribs.

Lochlan communicated only through sharp, staccato hand signals, pointing out thermal vents and jagged rock formations to avoid. The darkness was absolute, broken only by the pale blue glow of our weapons.

A deep, rhythmic vibration traveled through the water. It sounded like massive boulders grinding together. I halted my kick cycle, treading water as I peered into the black void. A shadow—something massive and formless—seemed to shift just outside the ring of my staff's light.

I spun around to signal Chaos.

The water behind me was empty.

Panic flared in my chest. "Chaos!" I screamed, the sound muffled and distorted through the rebreather.

Lochlan shot me a furious, wide-eyed glare, violently slashing his hand across his throat to signal silence.

I kicked backward, preparing to swim up his trail.

Before I could complete the motion, something cold, jagged, and impossibly strong clamped around my right ankle. In a fraction of a second, I was violently yanked down into the pitch-black abyss.

Chapter 9: The Abyssal Trench

The water violently displaced around me. Before my brain could register the shift in current, something freezing and textured like crushed glass clamped around my right ankle.

The kinetic snap of the pull nearly dislocated my knee. I was yanked straight down into the crushing black. Looking up, the pale blue glow of Lochlan's trident flared in the dark, then rapidly shrank into a meaningless pinprick as the abyss swallowed me.

My staff flared to life autonomously, casting a violent violet glow into the murky water.

It wasn't just a serpent. A mass of writhing, stone tentacles thrashed in the light, anchoring to a bulbous, heavily scaled mantle. Two massive, unblinking red eyes burned through the silt, locking onto me as a jagged, parrot-like beak snapped open just inches from my trapped leg.

I twisted wildly, kicking my free heel into the rubbery flesh of the tentacle, but the grip was like a hydraulic vice. The creature didn't slow. It was dragging me deeper, the ocean pressure building into a physical, crushing weight against my golden breastplate.

"Chaos!" I screamed, but the rebreather choked the sound into a pathetic, distorted gurgle. My lungs burned. The regulator was whining, pushed to its absolute limit by the speed of our descent.

Just as the darkness threatened to pull me under completely, the water above me boiled.

A streak of golden light shot past my visor like a torpedo. Chaos. His starlight blade didn't just cut; the superheated plasma instantly vaporized the water it touched, leaving a trail of furious white bubbles as it severed the tentacle wrapped around my leg.

The beast released a guttural, vibrating shockwave of pain that rattled my teeth.

I kicked free, fighting the disorientation to right myself. Above us, Lochlan dropped into the fray, his trident crackling with aquatic energy. But the beast ignored him. Its burning red eyes and remaining tentacles were fixated entirely on

Chaos, overwhelming his guard with a flurry of massive, heavy strikes.

I needed to break its focus. I couldn't risk a direct kinetic blast with Chaos so close to the beast. I pointed my staff toward the sheer, jagged wall of the trench looming to our right.

I channeled the energy, feeling the violent hum in my gauntlets, and fired.

The violet pulse slammed into the basalt. The trench wall detonated. A massive shockwave ripped through the water, followed instantly by hundreds of tons of dislodged rock. The beast shrieked, its red eyes snapping toward me, but the concussive backdraft of the explosion caught me first.

I was thrown backward, tumbling head over heels into the dark. A blinding, impenetrable cloud of silt and pulverized stone swallowed the light.

When I finally stopped spinning, I was completely alone.

"Chaos?" I gasped into the rebreather. Silence. Just the heavy, oppressive rushing of water and settling debris.

I pushed through the thick mud cloud, using the violet glow of my staff to cut through the murk. The rockslide had scarred the trench, creating a treacherous, jagged labyrinth of new debris. I navigated the maze, my heart hammering against my ribs, calling their names into the void until my throat was raw.

A faint, metallic scraping sound reached my ears.

I kicked harder, orienting myself toward the noise. As I rounded a massive slab of fallen basalt, the violet light caught a gleam of gold. Chaos. A colossal boulder had pinned his lower half to the seabed. His hands were braced against the stone, his muscles straining, but he couldn't find the leverage to move it.

"I'm stuck!" his voice came through the comms, heavily muffled and strained.

I didn't hesitate. I swam to his side, driving the base of my staff into the seabed just beneath the boulder. I focused the energy, feeling the familiar, heavy pull of the kinetic tether. I wrenched the staff upward. The violet energy latched onto the rock, groaning against the sheer weight before lifting it just enough for Chaos to violently roll free.

"Lochlan," he gasped, rubbing his thigh as he grabbed his floating sword. "We have to go back."

We moved as one, kicking off the seabed and tearing back through the settling silt.

As the battle came back into view, the water was stained with dark, thick ink. Lochlan was swimming backward, his movements sluggish and exhausted. The beast lashed out. A tentacle, tipped with a jagged bone-spur, darted past his guard.

It pierced squarely through the center of his chest.

Lochlan's body seized. The crackling blue energy of his trident flickered, then died completely as the weapon slipped from his hands and plummeted into the dark. The beast discarded his lifeless body like trash.

The water around me felt like it was boiling. A hot, blinding rage flooded my system, overriding the cold.

Chaos didn't wait. He shot forward, a blur of golden armor and starlight, severing two tentacles in a single, devastating cross-slash. The beast recoiled, sluggish and bleeding heavily, trying to track his impossible speed.

It was my turn.

I swam upward, positioning myself directly above the creature. I pointed my staff at the unstable, jagged overhang of the cliff face directly behind the beast. I didn't hold back. I dumped every ounce of my rage and kinetic energy into the strike.

The blast shattered the entire upper shelf of the trench. A massive section of the continental plate broke loose, plummeting downward. The beast looked up just as thousands of tons of rock slammed into the seabed, burying it completely.

The shockwave knocked us both back. When the water finally settled, there was nothing left but a mountain of rubble and absolute silence.

We swam down to the wreckage, the glow of our weapons cutting through the dark. We spent what felt like hours moving stones and searching the silt, desperate to recover Lochlan's body to return him to his people. But the abyss had claimed him.

"We mark these coordinates on the ship's telemetry," I said, my voice hollow, staring into the black water. "We'll come back with the Aquarians. They have the equipment to find him."

Chaos drifted next to me, his golden armor dull under the silt. "Agreed. The less time we spend down here, the better."

I gripped my staff, looking down the dark expanse of the trench. "If that was the guardian... the Tidal Trident should be somewhere under that rubble."

Chaos shook his head, his eyes scanning the deep path ahead. "No. It was heading somewhere."

"What do you mean?"

"Ambush predators like this don't eat in the open," Chaos grunted, wiping a layer of mud from his visor. "It was dragging you to its larder. I can tell you from experience, it grabbed me first when the lights went out. I cut its tentacle, so it went to the back of the pack for easier prey."

"Wait..." I mumbled, the realization dawning on me. "It grabbed you first?"

"Yeah," he said, turning to face down the trench. "Fortunately for me, I had my sword. Unfortunately for you, you were next in line."

"Ah," I deadpanned, giving him a hard look through the mask. "So that's why it came for me. You used me as bait."

"I prefer the term 'tactical diversion,'" Chaos teased, though the attempt at humor was heavy with the exhaustion of the fight.

Without another word, we turned our backs on the rubble and swam deeper into the abyss, following the invisible trail the monster had intended to drag me down.

Chapter 10: The Trident's Deception

The abyss squeezed my ribs, threatening to crush the air right out of my mechanical rebreather. Each kick of my legs felt like moving through wet cement, a humiliating contrast to the effortless, liquid speed the Aquarians possessed. I glanced back, using the violet glow of my staff to track the golden gleam of Chaos's armor. The deeper we swam, the heavier the silence became, broken only by the rhythmic, mechanical hiss of our recycled breath.

Then, the water began to whisper.

Gaia...

I whipped around, my staff carving a violet arc through the water. Nothing. Just the crushing, inky blackness.

You failed them...

The voice didn't come through the comms. It scraped against the inside of my skull, dripping with venomous accusation. I clamped my free hand over my helmet, but it did nothing to muffle the sound.

Chaos swam up beside me, his brow furrowed behind his visor, his hands signing a quick, silent question. I shook my head, my throat seizing in a sudden, icy panic. I tapped the side of my helmet, signaling a pressure glitch.

But the glitch didn't stop. The hissing water morphed into the deafening roar of plasma fire.

Flashes of bruised crimson and shattered glass superimposed themselves over the pitch-black ocean. I couldn't tell where the freezing water ended and the phantom heat of Talon began. The taste of ash flooded my mouth, choking out the recycled oxygen. Disembodied voices screamed my name, blaming me as the colony burned. Through the swirling, illusory smoke, Lochlan's pale, lifeless face floated up from the silt, his dead eyes locking onto mine.

A hard, golden grip clamped onto my bicep.

The physical jolt shattered the illusion. I gasped, choking on the air from the rebreather. Chaos floated directly in front of me, his dark eyes fierce and anchored. He didn't let go, his thumb pressing hard against my armor, physically grounding me against the crushing weight of the hallucinations. I clung to his arm, forcing my frantic heartbeat to match the slow, deliberate rhythm of his breathing until the burning colony faded back into cold water.

We pressed onward, following the trench until the jagged rock wall smoothed into a perfectly symmetrical, circular aperture.

We kicked into the tunnel. The oppressive ocean current died instantly, replaced by dead, stagnant water as the path sloped steeply upward. Minutes later, my helmet breached the surface.

I hit the quick-release on my jawline and ripped the rebreather off, gasping. The air was stale, tasting heavily of cold stone and ancient dust. Chaos broke the surface beside me, tapping the biometric display on his golden gauntlet.

"Atmosphere is breathable," he grunted, hauling his armored frame over the edge of the water and onto a solid cavern floor.

I pulled myself up beside him, water cascading off my breastplate. "Did that path feel engineered to you?" I asked, wiping brine from my eyes.

"The fact that it perfectly mirrors the corridors of the first Theian site?" Chaos said, shaking water from his hair. "Or the fact that it ended in a pressurized, breathable cavern at the bottom of the ocean? Yeah. Definitely engineered."

I stood up, shaking out my cramped legs. In the distance, a faint, pulsing luminescence bled through the dark. "Chaos, look."

We moved quickly across the cavern floor, the light growing brighter with every step. Half-buried in the jagged rock was a massive, seamless plasmetal edifice.

Unlike the armory, the lintel above these doors was completely blank. No runes. No warnings. The ambient static in the air made the hairs on the back of my neck stand on end. As we stepped within striking distance of the doors, the dormant biometric scanners recognized our Theian DNA.

The blank stone above the door didn't just illuminate; it sloughed off a layer of holographic camouflage. A single, stark word burned into my vision, translated instantly by the network sync in my skull.

Malevolent.

A wave of cold dread washed the remaining warmth from my blood. I looked at Chaos. His jaw was set tight, his hand resting instinctively on the hilt of his starlight blade. With a low, grinding groan of unseen mechanisms, the massive plasmetal doors began to part. The air that rushed out of the threshold didn't smell sterile. It smelled of decay and sinister, vibrating energy.

We stepped inside, the heavy thud of our boots echoing down a vast, vaulted corridor.

The walls here were a sprawling canvas of deep, jagged engravings. The violet light of my staff caught the edges of the carvings, bringing the ancient history to life. We walked slowly, our eyes tracing the rise and fall of forgotten civilizations, all brought to ash by a swirling, consuming vortex of darkness.

But as we ventured deeper, the narrative shifted. A panel depicted a small band of warriors, clad in armor identical to ours, standing defiant against the gloom. One of them held a massive trident.

I stopped walking. I stared at the etching of the trident, the ambient static in the room suddenly making it hard to breathe.

They weren't using the trident to strike the darkness. They were driving it into the earth. They were using it to pin the vortex.

It wasn't just a weapon. It was a lock.

My blood ran cold. The jagged pieces of the puzzle slammed together with a sickening, violent clarity.

We have guarded secrets beneath these waves for millennia. Knowledge passed down through generations. Thalassa's voice echoed in my memory.

How did a deep-sea civilization on Genesis know the surface-world legends of a Theian sorceress? Why were their scouts waiting exactly where the Arkenon sank?

These buildings only open for Theian DNA.

They couldn't breach this cavern. They couldn't open these doors. They had been guarding this trench for thousands of years, waiting for the key to fall from the sky. Tartarus hadn't sent us here to arm ourselves. The Aquarians hadn't sent us here to find a weapon.

They sent us here to unwittingly unbind the very darkness our ancestors had locked away.

The corridor opened into a gaping, shadowed threshold, radiating an energy that promised to swallow us whole. Chaos stepped up beside me, the starlight blade humming as he drew it from its sheath. His eyes narrowed, scanning the dark.

"Something's wrong," he rumbled, his voice low and dangerous. "I don't trust this."

I stared into the abyss, my fingers strangling the wood of my staff. "We didn't find an armory," I whispered, the crushing weight of the deception finally settling over me. "We walked right into a cage."

Chapter 11: The Shadow's Revelation

"We've been played," I whispered, the words hanging like a death sentence in the cold, echoing chamber.

Chaos's hand tightened around the grip of his starlight blade, the leather creaking under the strain. "Played? You think the Aquarians want us to unleash whatever is locked in here?"

I backed away from the towering, ominous doorway, my heart hammering against my golden breastplate. "It's the only thing that makes sense. They had scouts waiting exactly where we crashed. They handed over their deepest, most guarded secrets without a fight. How would they even know about Ayin? Her reign ended on a world that no longer exists... unless she told them."

Chaos’s eyes narrowed, scanning the dark. "Are they descendants?"

The stagnant air in the corridor violently snapped.

A localized vacuum popped my ears. A blur of pale skin and sleek, sub-dermal armor tore past us, moving with a liquid, impossible speed that defied the cavern's gravity. The Aquarian scout didn't look at us. He shot straight toward the glowing pedestal positioned just before the massive doors.

"No!" I screamed, thrusting my staff forward to unleash a kinetic blast.

I was a fraction of a second too late.

The Aquarian plunged his webbed hand directly into the center of the pedestal.

A blinding, oceanic blue light erupted outward as his fingers wrapped around the hilt of the Tidal Trident. The moment the weapon was dislodged, a concussive shockwave of raw energy detonated, throwing Chaos and me backward onto the hard stone floor.

A tortured, subterranean groan vibrated through my teeth. The massive plasmetal doors behind the pedestal didn't slide open smoothly. They shrieked, the sound of ancient metal grinding against an encrusted prison, peeling apart milliliter by milliliter. The noise was unbearable, driving me to cover my ears.

A sickly, bruised light began to bleed from the widening crack.

The ancient carvings on the cavern walls suddenly lost their rigid forms. The etched lines of stone liquefied, writhing and twisting like black ink in water. From the floorboards, towering, indistinct silhouettes detached themselves from the physical world. The shadows coalesced, swirling into a blindingly fast, protective cyclone of pure darkness around Chaos and me.

I reached out, trying to find the golden gleam of Chaos's armor, but the darkness was absolute. The grinding of the doors, the blue light of the Trident, the sickening energy of the prison—it was all swallowed by a terrifying, soundless void.

Then, gravity inverted.

My boots hit solid ground with a heavy thud. My vision tore back into existence, but the oppressive, decaying walls of the trench cavern were gone.

We stood on a jagged plain of floating stone. Above us, there was no cavern ceiling, only a swirling, bruised nebula of shadows and faint, distant starlight. My rebreather mask dissolved into fine black ash, blowing away in a wind I couldn't feel. Chaos materialized beside me, his blade already drawn and humming, his eyes wide as he took in the impossible landscape.

Before us stood a towering entity. He wasn't wearing armor; he seemed woven directly from the fabric of the void. His physical form constantly rippled, shedding smoke and drinking in the ambient light. Only his eyes were entirely solid—twin orbs of intense, piercing silver that locked onto me like a physical weight.

"Welcome, Theians," the figure spoke. The voice didn't travel through the air; it resonated directly within the marrow of my bones. "I am Azrael, King of Shadows. And this is my domain."

Chaos stepped in front of me, his starlight blade cutting a bright arc through the gloom. "What is this? Where is the Trident?"

The Shadow King chuckled, a dry, rasping sound devoid of any warmth. "Patience, warrior. All will be revealed in due time."

Azrael raised a long, narrow finger. The stone plain beneath us violently shifted, raising jagged pillars of dark stone to form a claustrophobic, makeshift arena.

"But since you insist on holding that blade," Azrael's silver eyes flared, "let us test your worthiness."

"What are you waiting for?" the voice whispered directly into my right ear.

I spun, throwing a devastating, kinetic-charged elbow strike. It connected with nothing but cold vapor.

Chaos lunged to my left, his sword slicing cleanly through Azrael's torso, but the Shadow King instantly dissipated, reforming ten feet away. He moved without kinetic resistance. He was playing with us.

"You rely on your eyes, Theians," Azrael taunted from the dark. "Eyes can be deceived."

Suddenly, the shadows around me shifted. The stone floor turned into the burning, blood-soaked streets of Talon. I heard the screams. I saw Lochlan's dead, pale eyes floating in the smoke, blaming me for his demise. My breath hitched. Panic flooded my chest, paralyzing my grip on my staff.

A shadow-construct of a raptor lunged for my blind spot.

I couldn't move. But Chaos did. He threw himself into the path of the strike, taking a glancing, violent blow to his golden pauldron to completely shield me from the attack.

Don't look, I commanded myself, forcing my eyes shut. Feel.

I stopped searching for a physical body and reached out with my energy, seeking the dense, cold resonance of Azrael's mass. There. A void in the static.

I dropped to one knee and swept my staff in a wide, kinetic arc, not aiming for where he was, but where the cold void was shifting. The blast connected. Azrael’s form rippled violently, forced backward as Chaos seamlessly capitalized on my strike, driving his blade within an inch of the King’s throat.

The shadows froze. The burning illusions of Talon dissolved into black mist.

Azrael did not reform to attack. He simply stood, looking at the glowing edge of

Chaos's blade, a faint glimmer of profound respect shining in his silver eyes.

"You fight as one," Azrael conceded, his voice dropping an octave. "When the illusion fractured your mind, Gaia, your warrior overcompensated to absorb the physical penalty. Your connection is highly resilient. That is a rare and remarkable weapon."

Chaos didn't lower his sword. "Explain yourself."

Azrael's tone turned deadly serious. "You must understand exactly what the Aquarians just unleashed. Ayin is not a mere sorceress. She is a Guardian of Divinity."

The title hit me like a physical blow. The childhood myths were real. Entities tasked with holding the very fabric of the universe together.

"If she is a Guardian," I breathed, "why did she destroy our world?"

"Because she harbors a profound, insatiable hunger for absolute control," Azrael answered, the shadows around him writhing angrily. "By imprisoning her cosmic counterpart, she ruptured the balance of the deities. She absorbed the vacuum, elevating her own strength to terrifying dominance. Some believe she may have been the very first."

A suffocating dread settled in my stomach. If Ayin was a god who had consumed another god, we were nothing but dust in her path.

"Do not succumb to despair," Azrael commanded, stepping closer. "She can be stopped. Ayin harbors a single, fatal flaw: her own staggering hubris. She believes herself utterly insurmountable. Because of this, she rarely exerts her full strength. She prefers to toy with her prey, savoring their psychological torment."

He pointed a shadowy finger at Chaos's blade. "You cannot overpower her through brute force. Her might is beyond measure. You must exploit her arrogance. Anticipate her cruel games, survive her illusions, and strike decisively when she believes you are already broken."

Azrael turned his silver gaze back to me. "The Tidal Trident is not merely a weapon. It is a conduit. It amplifies the inherent divinity within a being, allowing them to channel cosmic energies. It was forged by the other Guardians specifically to seal her away. But it requires a pure heart and a powerful will to unlock."

"The Aquarians knew," Chaos growled, his golden armor clinking as he lowered his blade. "They sent us down here to crack the lock for them."

"Projections of Ayin's power bled through her prison for millennia," Azrael confirmed. "She manipulated the aquatic civilization through their proximity to the trench. The prophecies they revere were authored by Ayin's whispers. They were pawns, maneuvering the true key—your Theian blood—to the door."

"So she's free," I whispered.

"She is waking," Azrael corrected. "Her first priority will be hunting the remaining Guardians who forged her prison. That will buy you a fraction of time. You must recover the Trident from the thief, and you must prepare."

He raised both of his narrow hands. The shadows condensed into two solid, glowing Spirit Crystals, hovering in the space between us.

"The Trident amplifies power, but it demands a great price," Azrael warned. "Ayin feeds on fractured loyalties and internal discord. To defeat her, you must conquer the shadows within yourselves. You must be whole."

Chaos stepped close, his shoulder brushing mine, a silent, unyielding wall of support. "We will be," he promised.

Azrael gave a slow, nearly imperceptible nod. "Take the crystals. Their power is symbiotic. As your bond and mastery increase, so will their amplification."

I reached out, my golden gauntlet wrapping around the warm, pulsing stone. The moment my skin made contact with the crystal, the stone plain began to dissolve beneath my boots.

"Never speak of this conversation," Azrael's voice began to fade into the rushing static of the collapsing realm. "Do not speak of my existence to anyone."

The shadows violently surged,

rushing up to devour my vision entirely.

"Or Death will find you."

Chapter 12: An Uneasy Alliance

The sharp, metallic scent of the Shadow Realm was gone, replaced by the damp, briny sweetness of filtered ocean water.

I groaned, squeezing my eyes shut as blinding, bioluminescent light pierced my retinas. My skull throbbed in punishing rhythm with my heartbeat. I pushed myself up, expecting my gauntlets to scrape against jagged stone, but they sank into a soft, woven kelp-silk cushion.

Beside me, Chaos bolted upright. His starlight blade was instantly in his hand, a low, dangerous hum filling the room as he swept the perimeter.

But there was no threat. We were back inside the serene, glowing coral walls of Siren's Hollow. Aquarian attendants floated past the open archways, completely ignoring the drawn weapon.

A young Aquarian with flowing mahogany hair stepped into the chamber, carrying a tray of pale, glowing fruit. She didn't flinch at Chaos's blade. "Welcome back," she chimed, her melodic voice grating against my headache. "A perimeter patrol found you unconscious near the trench shelf. We brought you here to recover."

I lowered Chaos's sword arm with a gentle press of my hand, keeping my eyes locked on her gills. "Found us?" My throat was parched. "The trench... the doorway..."

Her smile was perfectly, unnervingly serene. "The deep currents can induce severe nitrogen narcosis in surface dwellers. Your minds simply played tricks on you."

She set the tray down. "But you succeeded. We are eternally grateful that you recovered the Tidal Trident for us. It is a sacred relic, and we will ensure its absolute protection."

My jaw clamped shut. I didn't look at Chaos, but I could feel the heat radiating off his golden armor.

Recovered it for them? They had a scout tailing us. They let us trigger the trap, and then they stole the prize. We were sitting in the center of their metropolis, vastly outnumbered. If we called her a liar, we'd never make it out of the dome.

"Thank you," I forced the words out, keeping my face blank. "For everything."

Over the next few hours, we played the role of grateful, recovering guests. The Aquarians fed us, offered fresh tunics over our armor, and escorted us to a massive, pressurized docking bay at the edge of the city.

The Arkenon sat on the central landing pad, but its battered hull was completely encased in a shimmering, aquamarine energy field.

"Our engineers took the liberty of modifying your vessel," our escort explained, waving a webbed hand toward the ship. "The hydro-shield resists extreme deep-sea pressure. It is our gift to you, for returning our relic."

I stared at the glowing blue barrier. It wasn't just a shield. It was a leash. They were giving us the exact tools we needed to leave quietly. But if Ayin was free, why wasn't the ocean boiling? Why was the city so calm? Had Azrael just been a hallucination?

"Gaia. Chaos."

The voice echoed off the high, curved walls of the docking bay. I spun around, my staff dropping instinctively into my grip. My blood ran completely cold.

Lochlan was walking toward us. He wasn't pale and lifeless in the silt. He didn't have a massive, jagged hole straight through his chest. He was wearing fresh ceremonial robes, moving with a stiff, guarded limp.

"Lochlan," Chaos growled, stepping in front of me. "You took a bone-spur through the heart."

Lochlan stopped, his pale eyes darting toward the Aquarian guards stationed at the far end of the bay. He lowered his voice to a strained whisper. "I remember the strike. I remember the cold. Then... nothing. I woke up in a medical ward three hours ago without a single scratch on me." He rubbed the center of his chest, a violent shudder ripping through his shoulders.

"They won't tell me what happened," he continued, stepping closer to the Arkenon. "They just smile and offer food. It's suffocating. And the Trident—they claim it's 'secure,' but they locked it in the deepest vault beneath the High Council's chamber. It's completely barricaded behind a localized pressure barrier."

He looked at us, his face tight with urgency. "If it was a weapon meant to defend the city, Thalassa would have it in the throne room. They're hiding it. And I don't think they're hiding it to protect us. We have to get it back."

My fingers slipped down the smooth wood of my staff until they brushed the cold, hard facet of the Spirit Crystal Azrael had given me. It pulsed against my palm—a heavy, undeniable resonance.

I wasn't crazy. The Shadow King was real. The sorceress was waking up. And the Aquarians were pawns, holding the key locked away until she came to collect it.

I looked at Chaos. He gave a sharp, single nod. We had to trust the dead man.

"They didn't protect the relic, Lochlan," I kept my voice dead-level, hiding the tremor in my chest. "They used us to open a prison. The Trident was the lock."

I rapidly broke down the encounter at the cavern, the scout who stole the weapon, and Tartarus’s warning about Ayin. I honored my promise to Azrael, keeping the Shadow King's existence out of the story, but I let the full weight of the sorceress's release settle between us.

Lochlan’s pale skin turned completely translucent. He stared at the floor, processing the absolute betrayal of his own council. "If she wakes... she'll tear Siren's Hollow apart just to get her key back." He looked up, his eyes hardening into flint. "We have to steal it first."

"We can't break a high-council vault alone," Chaos stated, his eyes coldly calculating the tactical angles. "Not without bringing the entire city guard down on us."

"We need a distraction," I said, looking up at the shielded hull of the Arkenon. "We need an army. Kameel offered the Repterians' help. If we can get back to the surface, we can coordinate with Tartarus and bring a strike force."

Lochlan nodded, stepping past us toward the boarding ramp. "Then we leave now. We play the grateful surface-dwellers, test this new shield, and break the surface."

He turned back, his expression grim.

"Then... we prepare for war."

Chapter 13: The Repterian Pact

The Arkenon's landing gear sank deep into the sprawling, root-choked mud of the Repterian kingdom. The air that rushed through the open hatch was suffocatingly thick, heavy with the scent of rotting earth and strange, sickly-sweet blossoms.

Before the ramp even touched the ground, we were surrounded.

A dozen Repterian soldiers emerged seamlessly from the dense foliage, their spears lowered, their slitted eyes tracking our every movement.

Lochlan’s hands white-knuckled the ship's bulkhead. His pale skin looked almost translucent in the murky green light of the swamp. "They aren't exactly fans of surface-dwellers," he swallowed hard, his gills flaring in distress. "It might be best if I stay and... guard the ship."

Chaos and I exchanged a flat look. Leaving the Aquarian alone with our only ride out of here wasn't an option, but dragging a terrified man into an apex predator's camp was a liability.

"Stay out of sight," I told him, stepping past him onto the ramp. "Lock the hatch behind us."

Chaos and I descended into the mud. The soldiers didn't speak. They simply fell into a tight, flanking formation, escorting us down a narrow, winding path carved through the dense interior of the jungle. Above us, the canopy erupted with the strange, melodic clicks and shrieks of hidden wildlife.

The vegetation suddenly broke, revealing a sprawling settlement woven directly into the massive roots of the ancient trees. Vibrant stone and timber huts lined the path. The low, rhythmic thumping of drums and the distant sound of children's laughter bled through the humid air.

At the center of a wide communal courtyard stood a massive, awning-shaded structure.

Inside, the air was remarkably cool. Sitting upon a throne of woven, iron-hard vines was Chief Drazil. He was a mountain of a reptilian, his chest broad and covered in thick, dark scales. His piercing yellow eyes locked onto us with the heavy, unblinking stillness of a striking serpent. Beside him stood a younger female wearing a polished bone tiara, her gaze sharp and curious. Princess Gwana.

"Theians," Drazil's voice was a deep, chest-rattling rumble that vibrated the floorboards. "I am Chief Drazil. My daughter, Gwana. Kameel has spoken of your... disruptions in the temple."

I didn't waste time on pleasantries. I stepped forward, holding my staff. "Chief Drazil, we are out of time."

I laid it all out. I told him about the cavern in the Abyssal Trench. The Aquarians' deception. The Tidal Trident, and the slumbering god of destruction it had just unchained.

Drazil sat perfectly still, absorbing the weight of the universe cracking open. "We have long distrusted the Aquarians," he finally rumbled, his claws slowly tapping the armrest of his throne. "They play a dangerous game with forces they do not understand. We will not stand idly by while the oceans boil."

He leaned to his side, whispering a low string of guttural clicks to Gwana. She offered a sharp nod and darted out through a side passage.

"You do not need an army for a vault," Drazil continued, his yellow eyes narrowing. "You need a scalpel. I am giving you my finest."

The heavy woven tapestry at the entrance shifted. Princess Gwana returned, leading four distinct warriors into the hall.

Kameel was at the front, offering a respectful dip of his head. Seeing a familiar face in the hostile camp sent a wave of relief through my chest.

"My brother, Leon," Kameel hissed, gesturing to the Repterian beside him. Leon was leaner, his scales shimmering with an iridescent, camouflaging green. He moved without making a single sound against the stone floor.

"Gex," Drazil rumbled. A heavily muscled brute stepped forward, his scales crisscrossed with thick, white scars. The ambient air felt heavier just with him in the room. "An expert in security and... forceful infiltration."

"And Poizen," Drazil finished. A sleek, vibrant female glided forward. Her scales bore bright, warning patterns, and her eyes were the color of crushed amethyst. "Her toxins can paralyze the leviathans of the deep."

"We are honored," I started, but a sudden commotion at the entrance cut me off.

A scout scurried into the hall, dropping to one knee beside the Chief and whispering frantically. Drazil's expression darkened.

"Before we finalize this pact," Drazil's voice cut through the tension like a blade, "there is a complication. Guards. Bring him in."

My stomach plummeted.

Two soldiers dragged a thrashing figure through the tapestry doors and threw him onto the stone floor. Lochlan. His pale face was covered in swamp mud, and he was trembling violently under the predatory gaze of the entire room.

"We found the Aquarian cowering in the landing struts of your vessel," Drazil stated, his tone dangerously flat.

I stepped smoothly between the spears and Lochlan. "He is with us, Chief. He was apprehensive about entering your territory given the history between your peoples. He panicked."

Chaos crossed his arms, the golden armor shifting. "He was terrified of you before," Chaos smirked, casting a glance at the scarred brute, Gex. "Now he's probably going to need a change of pants."

Lochlan visibly winced, a faint, embarrassed flush creeping up his pale neck.

Drazil grunted, his yellow eyes fixed on the trembling Aquarian. "Can he be trusted?"

"He held the line against an abyssal leviathan while we were pinned," I said, meeting the Chief's gaze without blinking. "He bled for us. And he knows exactly where the Aquarian High Council is hiding the Trident."

Drazil studied me for a long, heavy second. Finally, he clapped his massive hands together. The guards stepped back, releasing Lochlan.

"Our objective," I addressed the assembled squad, my voice echoing in the quiet hall, "is the Tidal Trident. It is buried deep within Siren's Hollow. But I need to be perfectly clear—we are not here to slaughter Aquarians. They are victims of Ayin's manipulation. This is an extraction, not a siege."

Lochlan pushed himself up from the floor, wiping the mud from his ceremonial robes. "It's locked in the Vault of Whispers," he explained, his voice shaky but gaining traction. "The room is encased in a localized pressure barrier powered by three separate hydro-conduits across the city. If we disable the conduits simultaneously, the vault opens."

I looked at the specialized squad. The tactical map was already forming in my head. "Lochlan, you navigate. Gex, you breach the conduits. Poizen, if we hit patrols, you put them to sleep quietly. Chaos and I will push straight for the vault."

"What about stealth?" Chaos asked, glancing at Kameel. "If the Aquarians see two humans in glowing gold armor, the entire city guard will descend on us."

Kameel hissed a low, clicking laugh. "We have that covered."

He tapped a rigid clasp on his collar. The ambient light immediately fractured around him, bending and swallowing his silhouette until nothing remained but the faint, displaced shimmer of the humid air.

"Perfect," I smiled, the adrenaline of the impending heist flaring in my blood. "We hit the conduits, crack the barrier, take the Trident, and extract back to the Arkenon."

Lochlan nodded. "We strike at first light. The majority of the city guard rotates shifts at dawn. It's our best window."

Drazil leaned back into his throne of vines, giving a slow, rumbling nod of approval. "Rest your bodies tonight, Theians. Tomorrow, you steal a god's key."

The humid air seemed to hold its breath as the sun sank below the canopy outside. I looked at Chaos, the invisible Kameel, and our trembling Aquarian navigator. The weight of Genesis pressed down on my shoulders, but for the first time since Talon fell, we weren't just surviving. We were fighting back.

Chapter 14: A Dark Reflection

Sleep offered no refuge. It was just a different kind of battlefield.

I stood in the ghost-streets of Talon. It wasn't the burning, screaming nightmare I usually endured. This was worse. It was dead silent.

The craters still bled heavy, noxious yellow fumes into the air, and the back of my throat tasted sharply of oxidized iron and blood. But the colonists were still here. Captain Delza stood near the skeletal remains of the command center. Dr. Rioma leaned against a shattered hab-wall. They didn't fight. They didn't bleed. They just watched me.

My boots crunched heavily over the charred plasteel debris as I walked between them. Every head in the settlement turned in perfect, mechanical unison, tracking my steps. Their mouths stretched open, the tendons in their necks straining as they shouted pleas, accusations, and curses—but no sound vibrated the air. The absolute silence was a physical, crushing pressure against my eardrums. Their eyes burned with the hollow, piercing weight of my failure.

And beneath that suffocating silence, a faint noise scraped across the ash.

It sounded like dry leaves skittering over cold stone. Laughter. Ayin’s laughter. The sound didn't come from the ruins; it was woven directly into the fabric of the silence, feeding on the drop in my stomach.

They are right, little Theian. You are a harbinger of ruin.

My heart hammered a violent, frantic rhythm against my breastplate. I opened my mouth to scream, to force the words out—we have a plan, Theia is real—but my vocal cords were paralyzed.

I looked down. The scorched earth beneath my boots was fracturing. Not from plasma fire, but from an impossible, bottomless depth. The cracks widened, swallowing the ash and revealing a sprawling, cosmic abyss of swirling starlight.

The silent figures of Talon didn't flinch as the ground gave way.

I fell. The freezing wind of the void ripped the stolen breath from my lungs. Below me, Genesis filled my vision, but it was tearing itself apart. The bruised oceans and sprawling emerald continents were violently peeling away from each other, splitting the planet down to the mantle.

On my left, the pristine, glass-and-plasmetal spires of Theia pulled away into the dark. On my right, a primal, magma-scorched wasteland roared with tectonic fury. In the expanding chasm between the two halves, the planet's core burned with a malevolent, pulsating heat.

Deep within that molten center, the colossal, segmented shadow of Umbra writhed.

I thrust my arms out, channeling every ounce of kinetic energy in my blood. I visualized the tether, visualizing my power wrapping around the planetary masses to pull them back together. But the energy vanished into the void. It felt like trying to stop a tidal wave with an open palm. The core burned brighter, blinding me, and I kept falling.

The void didn't end with a crash. It ended with a sharp, echoing click.

My boots hit a vast, perfectly smooth surface. The cosmic horror was gone. I was standing on an endless, sprawling chessboard of alternating stone and marble, bathed in the bruised starlight of Azrael's domain.

I stood on a black square. Across the board, towering silhouettes blotted out the stars. One was woven from shifting, smoking darkness—the King of Shadows. Beside him radiated a presence of ancient, suffocating malice. Ayin.

I snapped my head to the right. Chaos stood on a white square two spaces away. His golden armor gleamed, his starlight blade drawn, but he was completely paralyzed, frozen like a carved playing piece.

I tried to lunge toward him, but my boots were fused to the stone. I couldn't lift my heel.

A massive shadow detached itself from the far side of the board. A Knight, its form shifting and unstable, moved in jagged, right-angle leaps. The stone trembled as it landed on the square directly in front of me. Its featureless, smoking head tilted down. I felt the atmospheric pressure drop—a move had been made. It raised a jagged, light-swallowing lance and drove it straight down toward my chest.

I braced for the impact, my staff snapping into my grip.

But the lance never hit. The weapon dissolved into black smoke. The stone grid buckled, folding upward and hardening instantly into the smooth, seamless plasmetal of the Aquarian trench temple. I was standing directly in front of the colossal wall of inscriptions.

But the runes weren't dormant. They liquefied, crawling across the metal like black scarabs.

The translation burned its way into my skull with blinding lucidity. It wasn't a prophecy of redemption. It was a ledger of damnation. The etched warriors weren't pinning the darkness down; they were ripping the lock open.

"You see?"

I spun. Kameel stood beside me, but his yellow eyes were dilated with absolute terror. When he spoke, the guttural hiss of his voice was layered with the dry, skittering laughter of the sorceress.

"Your hands unchain the dark," Kameel/Ayin mocked, the dual voices scraping against my mind. "The Trident wasn't the lock. It was the key to my cage."

My eyes snapped open.

I tore myself off the woven-leaf pallet, my lungs violently expanding as I gasped for air. I wasn't smelling ash or ozone; the thick, earthy humidity of the Repterian swamp flooded my senses. Soft, gray pre-dawn light bled through the slatted wood of the hut.

I pulled my knees tight against my chest, shivering uncontrollably as cold sweat tracked down my spine.

Across the small hut, the rustle of gear broke the quiet. Chaos sat up from his own pallet, his dark eyes immediately scanning the room before locking onto me.

"Gaia?" he mumbled, his voice thick with sleep, but his posture already shifting into a protective guard. "Another one?"

I nodded slowly, my hands gripping my shins so hard my knuckles ached. The chessboard was gone. The void was gone. But the heavy, suffocating dread of the prophecy clung to my skin like ice.

Chapter 15: Siren's Hollow

The first hint of dawn bled a bruised lavender light through the Repterian canopy.

I stood at the base of the Arkenon’s ramp, rolling my shoulders to test the flex of the golden breastplate. The swamp was dead silent. The usual cacophony of the jungle had ceased, as if the entire ecosystem was holding its breath.

Kameel and Leon materialized from the mist, their iridescent scales muted in the low light. Gex followed, his heavy footfalls sinking into the mud, while Poizen quietly loaded a row of glass vials into her bandolier.

Lochlan gripped the edge of the ramp. His gills flared rapidly, his pale knuckles bone-white. "They aren't exactly fans of us," he swallowed, his voice tight. "It might be best if I stay on the ship."

Chaos didn't bother looking up from checking the seal on his gauntlets. "You're our map. You're walking."

Gex stepped forward, pulling a handful of small, translucent discs from a leather pouch. "Visual synchronizers," he rumbled, handing them to Chaos and me. "Press them over your retinas. They sync with our cloaking fields so you don't walk into our knives when we go invisible."

I pressed the cool, bio-luminescent membrane against my eye. It adhered instantly. Kameel tapped his collar, his physical form fracturing and disappearing into the ambient air. But through the lens, a faint, pulsing green thermal wireframe traced his outline.

The Arkenon lifted off, breaking the canopy and diving steeply toward the churning ocean. The newly integrated hydro-shield flared to life, encasing the hull in a protective, aquamarine bubble that hummed against the crushing pressure of the deep.

We glided seamlessly through the pressurized membrane of Siren's Hollow, the landing struts kissing the floor of a secluded docking bay.

The ramp lowered with a mechanical hiss. "Stay sharp," Lochlan whispered, stepping out into the bioluminescent glow of the city. "This place has eyes everywhere."

But as we moved through the winding coral archways, the streets were entirely empty. The usual hum of the metropolis was absent. There were no merchants in the plazas, no guards patrolling the suspended walkways. The silence was absolute, amplifying the heavy clack of Chaos's boots.

Lochlan’s brow furrowed, his eyes darting to the empty rooftops. "It's usually busier than this," he muttered over the comms. "Even at dawn. It's completely deserted."

A knot pulled tight in my stomach. Nothing about Ayin or her followers was ever easy.

We reached the first conduit nexus—a humming pillar of concentrated blue energy masked behind a decorative waterfall.

Kameel and Leon vanished, their green wireframes fanning out to secure the perimeter. Gex stepped up to the pillar. He didn't use a terminal. He drove his claws into the coral casing, ripping the panel free to expose a dense web of glowing energy lines. He pulled a specialized tool from his belt, his scarred hands moving with terrifying, surgical precision.

I gripped my staff, cold sweat bleeding down the back of my neck. Every click of Gex's tools echoed like a gunshot in the silent plaza. Beside him, Poizen hovered effortlessly, a venom-tipped dart gun raised as her amethyst eyes swept the dark alleys.

The blue pulse of the nexus suddenly flatlined. One down.

We repeated the grueling process three more times, navigating hidden service tunnels and maintenance access grates. Gex sliced through intricate locks and energy fields, killing the city's grid piece by piece.

But the eerie absence of the Aquarian guard gnawed at my nerves.

"Something is wrong," Lochlan insisted as we crossed a massive, empty courtyard. "We should have tripped a patrol by now."

Before I could answer, the courtyard narrowed into a colossal, spiraling shell structure. The Vault of Whispers. The massive archway, which should have been sealed by a blinding wall of pressurized water, stood completely open. Gex had killed the barrier.

"We did it?" Chaos murmured, stepping through the threshold, his starlight blade dormant but ready.

In the center of the dark vault, resting upon a raised dais of polished stone, sat the Tidal Trident.

It wasn't just metal; it looked as if it had been forged from the crushing pressure of the ocean itself. It pulsed with an inner, celestial blue light, casting long shadows across the walls.

I stepped up to the dais. The Spirit Crystal Azrael had given me, locked tightly into the wood of my staff, began to physically vibrate. It resonated with the

Trident, pulling at my golden gauntlets like a magnet. I reached out, my fingers wrapping around the frozen grip of the weapon.

A jolt of pure, cosmic energy shot up my arm, grounding my boots to the floor.

I lifted the Trident from the stone.

The exact moment the metal cleared the pedestal, the silence of Siren's Hollow shattered.

Deafening, bone-rattling klaxons erupted from every corner of the city. The soft bioluminescence of the coral died, violently replaced by spinning, arterial-red emergency lights. The grinding crash of heavy blast doors echoed through the courtyard outside, sealing off our escape routes.

"They knew!" Lochlan screamed over the sirens. "They let us open the vault!"

The ground shook. From hidden alcoves embedded in the vault walls, massive silhouettes ripped themselves free from the coral. They weren't Aquarians. They were colossal, automated defense constructs, built from reinforced, deep-sea shells and mechanized joints. Their single, massive optical sensors ignited with a blinding red glare.

"Defense constructs!" Lochlan shouted, backpedaling.

Chaos ignited his sword. The blade flooded the room with brilliant starlight. I spun the Trident in my right hand, feeling its immense weight balance perfectly against the staff in my left.

A red targeting laser painted the center of Kameel's chest.

"The cloaks aren't working!" Kameel hissed, deactivating the camouflage to save power as a beam of superheated energy instantly vaporized the stone where he had just stood. The constructs weren't tracking visual spectrums; they were tracking the cold-blooded thermal signatures of the Repterians.

They completely ignored Chaos, Lochlan, and me.

Gex roared, throwing his massive weight forward and slamming into the nearest robot, ripping a coral-plated arm clean off its chassis. Poizen vaulted off the wall, using her momentum to draw the targeting lasers away from Leon as he drove his daggers into a construct's exposed neck-joint.

But the armor was too thick. Another robot swatted Gex across the vault, slamming him into the stone wall. Before the machine could charge its weapon, Chaos descended from the shadows, his starlight blade cleanly severing the construct diagonally from shoulder to hip.

"We have to get back to the ship!" Chaos roared, ducking under a stray energy blast that boiled the water in the air.

We fought a brutal, tactical retreat. Gex and Chaos formed a rear-guard, using the severed chassis of the broken robots as heavy shields. Poizen and Leon cleared the high ground, dropping from the archways to disrupt the tracking sensors. I used the staff to throw localized kinetic shockwaves, knocking the machines off balance while

Lochlan navigated the maze of slamming blast doors.

We reached the docking bay. The primary entrance was sealed by a foot-thick iron bulkhead.

Chaos didn't stop. He drove his starlight blade directly into the seam of the doors. Superheated metal screamed, turning into molten, dripping slag as he carved a jagged triangle just large enough to squeeze through.

We threw ourselves into the bay, Gex ripping the slagged metal inward to seal the gap behind us. The massive constructs battered against the iron, unable to fit through the breach.

"We need the ship in the air, now!" I yelled, running up the ramp.

Poizen was already at the Arkenon's comms terminal, her hands flying across the controls to hack the local sensor grid. The ambient glow of her scales dulled as she stared at the main screen.

"Guys..." she breathed, stepping back. "You need to see this."

She threw the long-range telemetry onto the main display. Just beyond the upper edge of the city's atmospheric dome, the dark water was swarming with thousands of thermal signatures. Massive, armored war-submersibles.

The Repterian fleet. Chief Drazil had mobilized his entire army.

Lochlan’s face went completely ashen. "The city was empty because the Aquarian guard was already mobilizing at the roof of the dome to meet the fleet. They detected Drazil hours ago."

"It was a distraction," Kameel snarled, his claws gripping the console. "Drazil used us to breach the shields. He didn't know about the automated constructs."

A violent burst of static hijacked the Arkenon’s speakers. Thalassa’s voice filled the cabin, stripped entirely of its diplomatic warmth. It was absolute ice.

"To the intruders," the Chief Councilor announced, her voice echoing across the entire city grid. "Your act of aggression will not stand. We know Drazil’s assassins are within our walls. We know you have breached the vault. Surrender now, or face the full might of the deep."

The external hangar doors hummed, locking into place.

"Any vessel attempting to leave the dome will be forcibly boarded," Thalassa's voice promised. "If the relic, or any Repterians, are found aboard, the occupants will be executed. Surrender now, and your deaths will be swift."

The transmission cut to static.

"They'll check the flight logs," Lochlan whispered, staring at the locked hangar doors. "They know we were the last ship to land in this sector."

I looked down at the Tidal Trident in my hand, its blue light reflecting off my golden armor. The Repterians were trapped inside. The Arkenon was caged.

"How do we break out of a city," Poizen asked the silent room, "that just turned into a fortress?"

Chapter 16: Watery Labrinth

The jagged edges of the iron bulkhead still glowed a dull, cooling cherry-red where Chaos had carved our escape route. Outside the docking bay, the arterial-red emergency strobes of Siren's Hollow spun relentlessly, casting long, frantic shadows across the walls.

Thalassa's voice had stopped broadcasting, but the threat still hung thick in the air. Any vessel attempting to leave will be searched and destroyed.

Chaos's golden gauntlet collided with the bulkhead, denting the heavy iron. "We force our way out! We punch a hole straight through their dome and give them a taste of Theian strength they won't forget!" His starlight blade was already ignited in his other hand, casting a harsh white glare over his tense jaw.

"And face the entire defense grid head-on?" Kameel hissed, stepping out of the shadows. The optical camouflage was deactivated to save power, revealing the tight, pragmatic line of his reptilian mouth. "Those constructs completely ignored you, Chaos. They are programmed to exterminate Repterian thermal signatures. If we try to break the dome in that ship, they will turn the Arkenon into slag. Drazil's fleet is a distraction, yes, but it means every gun in this city is loaded and aimed upward."

"He's right," I said, stepping between Chaos and the door. "Save that anger for Ayin. The Aquarians are just guarding a cage they don't understand."

Leon leaned against the far wall, his iridescent scales blending into the dim lighting. "Stealth is our only viable vector."

"Stealth doesn't beat thermal scanners," Gex rumbled, his massive arms crossed over his scarred chest.

"We need a diversion," Poizen mused, her amethyst eyes flicking toward the Arkenon. "Something loud enough to pull every automated gun in the city toward the upper dome."

Every eye in the room shifted to Lochlan. The Aquarian looked pale, the bioluminescence of the city reflecting off the cold sweat on his forehead. "They'll check the flight logs," he swallowed hard, pacing the short span of the docking bay. "They know we were the last to land. The main thoroughfares and maintenance locks will be crawling with patrols..." He stopped, his gills flaring as his eyes widened. "Wait. The reclamation system."

Chaos narrowed his eyes. "What is that?"

"It's ancient. It predates the dome," Lochlan explained, his words spilling out rapidly. "It was built to filter and dump waste miles away from the city limits. It's a massive network of unlit, flooded tunnels that eventually vent to the surface. It was barricaded decades ago because... things from the deep kept crawling up through it."

Chaos scoffed, though his grip on his sword shifted. "We can handle deep-sea scavengers."

"It's not just the fauna," Lochlan warned. "It’s a labyrinth of methane and toxic decay. If we can reach the access hatch in the lowest, abandoned sector of the city, they will never think to track us through it."

"Gex and I can break a barricade," Chaos stated, the battle-light returning to his eyes.

Poizen unhooked a leather bandolier of vials from her hip. "And my toxins are not solely for combat. I carry filtration salves and pheromone masks."

I looked at the assembled squad. Four apex predators, a rogue Aquarian, and two Theians carrying a stolen god-key. "We have our path," I decided, turning to Lochlan. "The Arkenon came in with three crew members. It needs to leave with three crew members."

Lochlan looked at the ship, then back at me. "I can fly her. But the scanners will know I'm alone."

I gripped my staff. The Spirit Crystal Azrael had given me thrummed warmly against the wood. "Not if I leave a ghost behind."

I walked up the ramp and stepped into the cockpit. Drawing on the heavy, ambient static of the Trident strapped to Gex's back, I channeled a surge of pure kinetic energy through my staff. I didn't blast the console; I fractured the light around the pilot and co-pilot seats. Two shimmering, thermal-dense holographic projections of Chaos and myself materialized in the chairs.

"That will fool their internal biometrics long enough for you to break the dome," I told Lochlan, stepping back down the ramp. "Don't go straight to Drazil's fleet. Let the Aquarians chase you. We need them to think the Trident is still on that ship."

Lochlan nodded, his jaw set with a grim resolve. "I'll see you on the surface."

"Don't scratch the paint," Chaos grunted. "She's our only ride off this rock."

The ramp sealed shut. As the Arkenon fired its thrusters and lifted toward the open water lock, Kameel tapped his collar. The light bent around him and Leon, turning them into invisible, shimmering distortions. "We have a window," Kameel's disembodied voice hissed over our earpieces. "Move."

We slipped through the jagged hole in the bulkhead, leaving the docking bay behind.

Navigating the lowest sectors of Siren's Hollow felt like descending into a graveyard. The glowing, vibrant coral structures above gave way to rotting, calcified husks. The water pressure against the dome felt heavier here, the oppressive silence broken only by the distant, muffled concussions of Aquarian defense cannons firing at the Arkenon miles above us.

Kameel’s green wireframe halted in my visual lens. Before us sat a massive, circular iron hatch, completely fused to the wall by centuries of rust and calcification.

Gex stepped forward, handing the pulsing Tidal Trident to Kameel. Chaos drove the tip of his starlight blade into the hinges, the superheated plasma instantly boiling the water trapped in the rust. With the joints slagged, Gex and Chaos dug their armored fingers into the edges of the iron. The muscles in Gex's scarred back coiled as they hauled backward.

The hatch shrieked, tearing free from the wall and crashing onto the stone floor.

A wave of noxious air hit us like a physical blow. It smelled of sulfur, rotting marrow, and stagnant decay. I gagged, my eyes instantly watering.

Poizen moved swiftly, uncorking a small vial of thick, gray paste. "Smear this directly under your nose," she ordered, pressing a dollop onto my golden gauntlet. "It filters the airborne toxins and masks our scent."

I rubbed the bitter, eucalyptus-smelling paste over my upper lip. The nausea receded immediately.

We stepped into the gaping black maw of the reclamation tunnels. My staff provided the only light, a tight, violet beam cutting through the oppressive, dripping dark. The tunnel walls were slick with thick, bioluminescent slime, and the floor was submerged in knee-deep, freezing sludge.

We hadn't walked a mile before the sludge began to vibrate.

The water rippled. From the decaying debris along the walls, massive, multi-legged silhouettes ascended. Crabs the size of boulders, their carapaces covered in jagged barnacles, clicked their crushing pincers in the dark. Multiple pale, glowing eyes blinked erratically on their stalks.

"Hold your fire," Poizen whispered sharply. "They're blind. Those eyes don't see light; they read kinetic vibrations in the water."

Chaos didn't miss a beat. He stepped back, squared his shoulders, and delivered a devastating, armored punch directly into the tunnel's reinforced wall.

The seismic boom echoed down the corridor. The crabs instantly pivoted, scuttling furiously toward the source of the vibration. The moment their backs turned, Leon and Kameel dropped from the ceiling. Their daggers flashed in the dark, sliding effortlessly into the unarmored joints behind the creatures' heads, severing their brain stems before they could even screech.

We pushed forward, the tunnels growing narrower and more suffocating.

"Stop," Poizen commanded, throwing her arm out.

Blocking the entire width of the tunnel ahead was a dense, pulsating wall of fibrous fungus. It actively writhed, emitting a low hiss as corrosive, yellow spores drifted from its pores. Just standing ten feet away, the exposed skin on my face began to burn.

Poizen pulled a glass flask filled with a glowing, pale-blue liquid from her bandolier. "Drink a drop of this. It coats the throat against spore irritation."

I touched the vial to my lips. It tasted like liquid frost. Poizen then loaded a modified syringe into her dart gun and fired it directly into the center of the fungal mass. The chemical payload detonated into a fine mist. The fungus shrieked—a terrifying, almost organic sound—and violently recoiled, its tendrils shrinking back against the walls to reveal a jagged, narrow gap.

We squeezed through, the acidic slime hissing against our golden armor.

Fatigue began to gnaw at my bones. The heavy gravity of Genesis, combined with the suffocating atmosphere of the tunnels, made every step feel like walking through wet sand.

Then, a new sound bled out of the dark. A frantic, dry chittering that multiplied by the second, creating a high-frequency vibration against the soles of my boots.

Kameel's invisible silhouette froze. The beam of my staff illuminated a tidal wave of sickly green light pouring around the bend ahead.

Hundreds of insects, each the size of my fist, swarmed the tunnel floor and ceiling. Their multi-faceted eyes glowed with a toxic luminescence, and their needle-sharp mandibles clicked in a deafening, unified frenzy.

Before we could brace, the swarm hit us.

A heavy impact struck my shoulder. Needle-like mandibles bypassed the golden plating, sinking deep into the mesh beneath my arm. It felt like liquid fire was being injected directly into my vein. I cried out, tearing the insect off, but three more instantly took its place.

Gex roared in pain, slapping wildly at his thick, scarred arms. Chaos cursed, the starlight blade humming as he carved through the air, incinerating dozens of them in a flash of plasma, but the swarm simply flowed around the heat, latching onto his greaves.

"Don't let them break the skin!" Poizen yelled over the chaotic din, frantically tearing through her satchel. "The saliva is a neurotoxin! It paralyzes!"

My heart rate spiked. Paralysis down here meant being eaten alive in the dark.

Poizen pulled a wide-mouthed vial of dark, viscous liquid and dumped a shimmering pinch of silver powder into it. The concoction instantly frothed, turning violently volatile.

"Cover your mouths!" she screamed.

I clamped my gauntlet over my face just as she hurled the vial into the densest mass of the swarm.

The glass shattered. The liquid vaporized instantly, expanding into a massive, pungent cloud of acrid smoke that smelled intensely of scorched metal and burnt ozone.

The effect was devastating. The chittering warped into high-pitched squeals of agony. The insects released their grips, dropping from the walls and ceiling as their bioluminescence flickered and died. They blindly collided with each other, swarming backward in a panicked, disorganized retreat to escape the aerosol cloud.

Within seconds, the tunnel was empty, save for a few twitching husks on the floor.

I leaned heavily against my staff, my shoulder throbbing with a sickening, hot ache where the mandibles had pierced me. Poizen was immediately at my side, pressing a cooling, mint-scented balm directly into the puncture wounds. The burning subsided almost instantly.

"Deep-rot scavengers," she muttered, applying the same balm to a weeping bite on Gex’s arm. "The repellent will hold them off. But we need to move before the neurotoxin fully metabolizes."

We pushed through the chemical smoke, the tunnel eventually angling sharply upward.

"I found it," Leon's voice crackled over the comms, echoing from somewhere high above us.

The beam of my staff illuminated a vertical, metallic ventilation shaft stretching straight up into the pitch-black. The rungs were heavily oxidized, coated in thick, slippery moss. But drifting down the shaft was a faint, impossibly sweet current of cold, salty air.

"It's a tight fit," Chaos grunted, looking up the narrow tube. "I'll take the rear. I fill the entire hole. If anyone slips, you'll hit my armor before you fall back into that sludge."

The climb was agonizing. My thighs burned, and the golden gauntlets slipped against the wet, degrading iron. Above me, the Repterians scaled the shaft with terrifying, spider-like agility, completely unhindered by the vertical incline.

The air grew steadily colder. The stench of methane and rot was finally scrubbed away by the sharp, stinging smell of the open ocean.

A dim, circular sliver of starlight appeared above.

With one final, desperate heave, I pulled myself over the rusted lip of the vent and collapsed onto solid rock. I ripped my helmet off, gasping violently, letting the freezing night air fill my lungs.

We were sitting on a jagged, volcanic outcrop. Below us, the violent, crashing surf of the Genesis ocean battered the cliffs. Above us, the sprawling, bruised tapestry of the night sky stretched out unhindered by domes or cavern walls.

I looked down at the Tidal Trident, still glowing safely in Gex's scarred grip. We had survived the dark.

Chapter 17: Surface Negotiations

"Well, that was... invigorating," Chaos coughed, spitting a glob of stagnant tunnel water onto the volcanic rock. He rolled his shoulders, the golden armor grinding slightly as he worked a kink out of his back.

I leaned heavily on my staff, letting the freezing ocean wind strip the stench of methane from my skin. "You find anything that involves breaking things invigorating."

He wiped a smear of glowing green insect blood from his cheekplate, his signature smirk breaking through the grime. "Less thinking. More action."

Gex took a massive, chest-expanding breath, his scarred scales flexing in the moonlight. Leon dropped onto a nearby boulder, offering Poizen a respectful, silent dip of his head. Without her alchemical masks and neutralizing vapors, our lungs would have blistered miles below the surface.

"Eyes up," Kameel hissed, his slitted eyes fixed on the bruised horizon.

A low, rhythmic thrum vibrated the stones beneath my boots. Twin beams of harsh white light cut through the ocean mist. The Arkenon descended from the cloud layer, the aquamarine hydro-shield still flickering faintly across its hull. The landing struts hit the jagged cliffside with a heavy, metallic groan, and the ramp hissed open.

Lochlan practically fell out of the ship. His ceremonial robes were rumpled, and his gills flared in rapid, distressed rhythms. "I lost your transponders on the scanners the second you breached the lower sectors," he breathed, his wide eyes darting over our battered squad before locking onto the pulsing blue light of the Tidal Trident in Gex’s massive fist.

"We're in one piece," Chaos interrupted, stepping forward to meet him. "How did the extraction go?"

"The scanners bought the holograms," Lochlan said, running a trembling hand through his damp hair. "They cleared my exit, convinced the Trident was still inside the dome. But..." He swallowed hard, looking back toward the ship's comms array. "I intercepted the surface frequencies once I broke the water. Chief Drazil isn't responding to our extraction codes. He's ordering the Repterian fleet into a strict attack formation."

Lochlan looked directly at me, his pale face tight with fear. "He sounds... wrong, Gaia. Delusional. It's the exact same manic aggression the Aquarian High Council had."

The roaring ocean surf suddenly felt deafening. The cold dread in my stomach crystallized into absolute certainty. Ayin wasn't just manipulating the Aquarians from her encrusted prison. She was already inside Drazil's head. She was orchestrating a massive, localized war to mask her return to the surface.

"We have to intercept Drazil's flagship," I said, gripping my staff. The Spirit Crystal Azrael had given me flared warmly against my palm, responding to the spike of adrenaline in my blood. "If they fire on Siren's Hollow, the ocean turns into a graveyard."

"The fleet is running silent," Gex rumbled, his heavily muscled arms crossing over his chest. "Command is denying all incoming frequencies. They will treat any approaching vessel as hostile."

"Then we kick the door in," Chaos stated, marching up the ramp of the Arkenon. "We have a god-killing weapon. We force them to listen."

Poizen stepped into the harsh light of the ramp, her amethyst eyes calculating the tactical angles. "A targeted demonstration of the Trident's output could be... persuasive. A localized blast near the flagship's bow. Enough kinetic force to paralyze their advance without drawing blood."

"A calculated risk," Kameel hissed, his scales catching the ship's running lights.

"But a necessary escalation to halt a massacre."

"We board the flagship first," I decided, locking eyes with Chaos. "Get us through their defensive perimeter."

I turned to the elite squad. "Chaos and I will breach the command deck. We bring the Trident and force Drazil to stand down. Gex, Kameel, Leon, Poizen—hold the Arkenon in an exfiltration hover directly above the flagship. If Drazil refuses to listen, or if Ayin has completely corrupted him..."

Chaos drew his starlight blade a fraction of an inch, letting the superheated plasma hum in the quiet night. "We fire the warning shot."

Gex grunted his approval. Leon and Kameel fell into perfect, silent formation heading up the ramp.

I stood on the precipice for one last second, staring out over the churning black water. The wind felt malicious now, carrying an unseen, suffocating weight. The sorceress was awake, and she was already moving her pieces across the board. We weren't just racing to stop a war. We were flying directly into her trap.

Chapter 18: The Gathering Storm

The Arkenon's hydro-shield screamed as we leveled out, the hull skimming inches above the violent, black swells of the ocean.

I stood behind Chaos's pilot seat, my knuckles white as I gripped the Tidal Trident in my right hand and my staff in my left.

The ambient blue light of the Trident cast long, harsh shadows across the cockpit. Chaos wasn't making jokes. His jaw was locked, his eyes darting across the telemetry screens with a lethal, absolute focus.

The moment our sensors cleared the coastal interference, the cabin exploded with sound.

Deafening proximity klaxons blared. The central holographic tactical table violently flared to life. The projection of the dark ocean instantly drowned in a sea of arterial red.

"That is... a lot of red," Lochlan breathed, stepping up beside me, his pale face reflecting the bloody glow of the tactical map.

"It's Drazil's entire armada," Chaos confirmed, his thumbs hovering over the yoke's weapon toggles. "They're in a staggered blockade formation directly over the dome. He's anticipating a preemptive strike from the Aquarians."

Through the cockpit glass, the shadows of the Repterian warships began to blot out the starlight. Massive, predatory dreadnoughts hovered over the water, bristling with heavy plasma batteries and sleek, armored plating.

A sudden burst of static violently hijacked the Arkenon’s internal speakers. It wasn't just noise; it was a high-frequency screech that felt like ice picks driving into my eardrums.

"Both Repterian and Aquarian frequencies are completely jammed," Poizen yelled over the static, her hands flying across the auxiliary comms terminal. "There is a massive localized interference field bleeding into our receivers!"

My stomach plummeted. "Swap to the Theian encrypted network," I ordered, ripping open an emergency cache beneath the console and tossing sleek, stone comm-beads to the squad. "Our tech runs on a completely different quantum frequency. They can't jam this, but they won't be able to hear us either."

I pressed the bead into my ear. The excruciating static instantly vanished, replaced by the clean, silent hum of our private channel.

"I've isolated the interference," Poizen reported through the clear comms, her amethyst eyes wide as she stared at her monitor. "It's a localized energy pulse. Faint, but incredibly dense. And it's not Aquarian or Repterian."

"Where is it coming from?" I demanded.

"Deep," she whispered. "Directly beneath the bedrock of the Vault of Whispers. It's a repeating, sub-harmonic broadcast designed to scramble sensors and flood the local comms with aggressive static."

"Ayin," Chaos growled, his knuckles cracking as he gripped the yoke. "She’s not just waking up. She's accelerating the paranoia. She’s blinding both sides so they panic."

"She feeds on discord," I said, the crushing weight of the Shadow King's warning returning to my chest. "If neither side can communicate, the first one to flinch starts a massacre."

"Gaia," Kameel's voice hissed sharply over the comms. The invisible Repterian was tapping into the decrypted local traffic on his wrist-pad. "I sliced through the static on the Repterian short-wave. Listen to this."

He patched the audio into our earpieces.

It wasn't Drazil's deep, measured rumble. It was a chaotic overlap of aggressive, barking reptilian voices.

"...ignore the Chief's hold order. Target locks on the dome."

"Aquarian shields are fluctuating. Spin up the main plasma batteries now!"

"We end the fish today. Fire on my mark..."

"A mutiny," Leon stated flatly from the shadows of the cargo bay.

"Drazil is trying to hold the line," I realized, my blood running cold. "But Ayin's signal is amplifying the generations of distrust. His own generals are going rogue to claim dominance over Genesis."

"We need to get to Drazil's flagship. Now," Chaos barked, shoving the Arkenon’s thrusters to maximum. The G-force slammed me back against the bulkhead. "Brace yourselves. We are punching straight through the blockade."

"You are flying a straight line into a hot zone!" Gex roared over the whine of the engines. "We don't have active IFF tags! They will paint us as an Aquarian stealth bomber!"

"Let them try to hit us," Chaos snarled, the golden armor shifting as he threw the ship into a violent, evasive barrel roll.

The ocean below us churned as the thrusters kicked up massive walls of water.

The looming, jagged silhouette of Drazil's flagship dominated the center of the fleet.

A shrieking, high-pitched tone locked onto our console.

"Targeting lock!" Lochlan screamed. "We are painted!"

The sky outside the viewport instantly turned blinding white. A superheated pillar of plasma erupted from one of the rogue Repterian destroyers on our flank. It wasn't aimed at the dome—it was a warning shot that streaked mere inches across the Arkenon's bow, the sheer heat of it searing the ambient moisture in the air.

We didn't have time to exhale.

From the black depths of the ocean below, the water boiled. The automated defense constructs of Siren's Hollow—operating on their own lethal, uncompromising programming—registered the plasma fire as a direct assault on the dome.

A retaliatory beam of concentrated, oceanic energy erupted from the sea. It bypassed us completely and slammed dead-center into the hull of a Repterian frigate.

The explosion was catastrophic. The frigate's shields shattered like glass. The vessel buckled, its hull ripping apart in a fiery shockwave that illuminated the entire armada in apocalyptic orange. Flaming debris rained down into the boiling sea.

Chaos yanked the yoke, fighting the shockwave to keep the Arkenon from spinning out of control.

The sky tore open. The deafening roar of Repterian plasma cannons powering up echoed across the ocean, answered instantly by the rising, violent glow of the Aquarian defense grid beneath the waves.

The fragile, razor-thin line of peace had snapped.

We hovered in the direct center of the crossfire—a single, tiny transport ship holding the key to a god's cage, caught in the opening volley of a global war.

Chapter 19: A Diplomatic Minefield

A concussive shockwave slammed into the Arkenon, throwing me hard against the bulkhead. Outside the viewport, the night sky was torn apart by crisscrossing streaks of superheated plasma and blinding, oceanic energy beams.

Chaos fought the yoke, the muscles in his arms corded tight as he kept us hovering in the dead center of the crossfire.

"The flagship is hailing us!" Gex roared over the scream of our overtaxed hydro-shield, his scarred fingers tearing across the auxiliary comms. "It's a forced override on the local frequency!"

"Put him through!" Chaos shouted.

The central console flickered. A massive, slightly distorted hologram of Chief Drazil projected into the cramped space between the pilot seats. The audio feed that flooded our cabin was a chaotic maelstrom of blaring Repterian proximity alarms and barking officers.

Drazil’s thick scales bristled, his yellow eyes burning with unadulterated fury through the static. "They fire on my armada!" his voice rattled the speakers. "This is an act of war! Your 'manipulated' Aquarians are finally showing their true teeth!"

"Chief, you have to listen to me!" Chaos yelled back, not looking away from the viewport as he dodged a stray blast. "One of your destroyers broke formation! Your fleet fired the first shot! The

Aquarians' automated grid just returned fire!"

"You dare defend them?" Drazil snarled, leaning closer to his console so his holographic face loomed over us. "You tell me tales of an ancient, manipulating phantom! Where is this Ayin? Is she afraid to show herself? You expect me to fold my hand and retreat while my ships burn?"

I stepped directly into the holographic pickup radius, gripping my staff. "Chief Drazil, she is in your head!" I pleaded, raising my voice over the alarms. "We tracked a sub-harmonic energy pulse originating from beneath the dome. It's an interference field designed to amplify paranoia and jam your comms!"

"A convenient fiction, Theian."

Another figure stepped into the holographic projection beside Drazil. It was a Repterian general, his face heavily scarred, his eyes narrowed with lethal suspicion. "You bring us ghost stories while our warriors bleed. You are stalling. Trying to exploit our honor so we don't crush those underwater vermin once and for all!"

Kameel hissed from the shadows of the cargo bay. The rogue faction.

Drazil raised a massive hand, silencing the general. He turned his burning yellow eyes back to me. "And what of the Aquarian broadcasts, Gaia? They accuse you of aggression. They claim they have Repterian prisoners captured during your little infiltration!"

My stomach plummeted. The lie was so blatantly fabricated, yet Drazil believed it with every fiber of his being.

"Chief Drazil, they have no prisoners," I stated, keeping my voice dead-level. "Your team is standing right here."

I waved my hand. Kameel, Leon, Gex, and Poizen stepped fully into the light of the holopad.

Drazil’s projection visibly faltered. He stared at his elite squad, safe and unharmed aboard our vessel.

"Then why did they broadcast it?" Drazil thundered, turning his head to shout at the officers off-screen in his command center. "Generals! Roll call! Find out who is missing!"

Lochlan leaned into the comms pickup, his pale face illuminated by the blue light. "Chief Drazil, Thalassa’s broadcast never mentioned hostages. She only threatened to arrest anyone attempting to flee the dome."

"It's the rogue faction in your own ear, Chief!" Kameel hissed, stepping closer to the projection. "Your generals are feeding you false translations to force your hand!"

"They fired the first shot to trigger the defense grid!" Leon added.

Drazil froze. The horrific realization that his own council had orchestrated a mutiny began to crack the armored shell of his rage. He looked at the scarred general beside him.

But Ayin's poison ran too deep.

Before Drazil could issue a stand-down order, the Arkenon’s telemetry array screamed a deafening, continuous tone.

"Massive energy surge!" Poizen yelled, pointing at her monitor. "Directly below us! The Aquarian central defense nexus isn't just firing localized shots anymore. They are spinning up the primary grid for a full-scale barrage!"

The ocean beneath the Arkenon began to glow with a terrifying, radioactive blue intensity. The water literally started to boil.

"Chief, wait!" I screamed into the hologram. "We can stop this!"

But Drazil's eyes had already shifted back to his own tactical display. The momentary hesitation was gone, swallowed by cold, absolute war. "Too late, Theian," he growled. "The time for talk is over."

He slammed his massive fist down on a console out of frame. "All units! Break their dome! Unleash the fury of the Repterian Nation!"

The hologram violently cut out, plunging the cockpit back into the flashing red emergency lights.

A split second later, the sky tore open. Hundreds of Repterian plasma cannons fired in devastating, unified synchronization. A blinding wave of superheated destruction slammed into the ocean just as the Aquarian energy grid erupted upward.

The Arkenon was tossed like a leaf in a hurricane as the two massive nations collided, ripping Genesis apart.

Chapter 20: Crossroads of Fate

The Arkenon shuddered violently as another volley of Aquarian energy beams slammed into the distant Repterian lines, turning the night sky outside our viewport into a blinding grid of lethal light.

"The flagship is hailing us!" Gex roared over the scream of our overtaxed hydro-shield, his scarred fingers tearing across the auxiliary comms. "It's a forced override on the local frequency!"

"Put him through!" Chaos shouted, ripping the yoke hard to port to dodge a burst of flak.

The central console flickered. Through the static, the bridge of Drazil's flagship projected into our cockpit as a maelstrom of flashing crimson alarms. I watched his tactical officers scrambling in the background of the hologram.

Drazil's thick scales bristled, his yellow eyes burning with unadulterated fury. He slammed a massive fist onto his throne.

"They dare attack my fleet! This is an act of war! Your 'manipulated' Aquarians are showing their true intentions!"

"Chief, you have to listen!" Chaos yelled back, keeping his eyes locked on the chaotic sky outside. "One of your ships fired first! The Aquarian automated grid just returned fire! It's all being orchestrated by Ayin! We have the Trident. Fall back and regroup!"

Drazil's projection leaned closer, his eyes narrowing. "Ayin? You speak of an ancient, manipulating phantom! Why have we not seen her? Is she afraid to show herself? You expect me to fold my hand and retreat like a coward?"

I stepped directly into the holographic pickup radius, gripping my staff. "Chief Drazil, Poizen detected a sub-harmonic energy pulse originating from below the dome! It is actively interfering with both your comms and theirs, amplifying the distrust!"

"A convenient story, Theian."

Another figure stepped into the hologram beside Drazil. It was the scarred Repterian general from the council—the leader of the rogue faction. "You bring us mythical sorceresses while our warriors bleed. This is a weakness you attempt to exploit, to keep us from crushing these underwater vermin once and for all!"

Drazil raised a hand, silencing the general. He turned his burning eyes back to me. "And what of the Aquarian broadcasts? They accuse you of aggression. They claim they have Repterian prisoners, captured during your infiltration!"

My stomach plummeted. "Chief Drazil, they have no Repterian prisoners," I stated, my voice dead-level. I waved my hand, and Kameel, Leon, Gex, and Poizen stepped fully into the light of the holopad. "They are here. With us."

"Then why are the Aquarians claiming they do?" Drazil thundered, turning his head to shout at the officers off-screen. "Generals! Roll call! Find out who is missing!"

Lochlan leaned into the comms pickup. "There is no mention of prisoners on the Siren's Hollow broadcast, Chief."

"It's the rogue faction providing misinformation!" Kameel hissed at the hologram.

"I bet they fired the first shot, too!" Leon added.

Drazil froze. The horrifying realization that his own generals were feeding him lies began to crack the armored shell of his rage. But before he could issue a stand-down order, a deafening proximity klaxon blared through the Arkenon's cockpit.

"Massive thermal signature!" Poizen yelled, pointing at her monitor. "It broke the Aquarian lines!"

Through the viewport, the ocean boiled. A colossal Aquarian defense construct—four times the size of those we had fought in the vault—surged from the surf. Its massive optical sensor burned a menacing red as it locked directly onto

Drazil’s flagship, charging a devastating plasma volley.

"Shields failing!" a comms officer screamed through Drazil's holographic feed. "Central propulsion damaged! We're losing speed!"

"Gaia!" Chaos barked. "Can you do something about that massive autonomous weapon attacking Drazil's ship?"

"On it!" I yelled, turning and sprinting toward the cargo bay. "Opening the observation hatch! Keep us level!"

The wind nearly tore me off my feet as the heavy blast doors slid open. Freezing ocean spray pelted my golden armor.

"Wait," Poizen interjected over the squad channel, her tone sharp. "Earlier, you two seemed hesitant to demonstrate the Trident's power. Do you actually have no idea how to fire it?"

"Now is the time to find out!" Kameel hissed over the wind. "Make it a calculated strike, Gaia, or the Chief's ship is scrap!"

"Have faith in her," Chaos cut in smoothly, banking the Arkenon to give me a clear line of sight. "She has a special gift for figuring these things out."

I planted my boots onto the vibrating deck plating. I raised the Tidal Trident, feeling the Spirit Crystal on my back pulse in time with my racing heart. I aimed the heavy, pronged head down at the colossal machine.

Don't just hit it. Bind it.

I unleashed the energy. It wasn't a flash; it was a torrential geyser of compressed, cosmic blue light. The beam slammed into the construct. The water surrounding the machine instantly flash-froze into massive, jagged glacial spikes, locking its joints and completely paralyzing its core. The massive construct tipped backward, plunging lifelessly into the dark waves as Drazil's flagship soared safely overhead.

As the blue light faded from the Trident's prongs, a different resonance caught my attention. It was the faint, sub-harmonic pulse Poizen had isolated—Ayin's signal.

I drove the blunt end of the Trident into the deck and pushed my awareness outward, riding the cosmic frequency down into the bedrock.

The moment my mind touched the signal, a psychic shockwave shattered my focus. The physical world was overwritten by aggressive, violent hallucinations. I tasted burning coral and reptilian blood. I saw Drazil's fleet glassing the dome, and thousands of Aquarian bodies floating in the ash. I saw Repterian scales mounted on spikes.

These negative prophecies painted a bleak, terrifying landscape. Ayin wasn't just jamming the signals; her influence was a poisonous current actively injecting these nightmare visions into the minds of both armies.

I screamed, violently twisting the Trident to shatter the frequency. The feedback knocked me to my knees.

The localized jamming field snapped. Instantly, the Arkenon's comms flooded with unencrypted surface traffic.

"Chief Drazil!" Thalassa’s cold, imperial voice cut through the static, echoing across both armadas. "Your aggression will be met with overwhelming force. Withdraw, or your fleet will be annihilated. The Tidal Trident remains under our protection."

"You fish-folk do not scare me!" Drazil’s roar blasted back in real-time. "Release the Repterian prisoners or I will show you overwhelming force!"

"No!" I screamed into my comm, realizing the broken jammer meant they were finally hearing each other's poisoned lies.

Before I could broadcast the truth on an open channel, a shockwave of apocalyptic proportions hit the Arkenon. It wasn't energy fire. It was pure kinetic displacement.

The lights flickered and died as I scrambled back into the cockpit. Poizen, Gex, and the others were staring in absolute terror at the main viewport.

The ocean beneath us wasn't just boiling; it was parting.

A colossal entity erupted from the depths. Water cascaded like a waterfall off an immense, stone-scaled serpentine form. Massive, jagged spikes ran along its back and jawline. Two colossal, muscular arms ending in scythe-like claws breached the surf. Its glowing, malevolent red eyes burned through the dark, and its jaws unhinged to reveal hundreds of razor-sharp teeth.

It was the creature from the trench, but exponentially larger, mutated into a force of primal nature. It felt vaguely familiar, like a nightmare I couldn't quite place.

"What in the blazes is that?!" Poizen yelled, her composure completely shattered.

My blood ran to ice. "It must be... that protector," I whispered, the words scraping my dry throat. "From the Aquarian archives."

The leviathan unleashed a deafening, localized roar that physically cracked the Arkenon's viewport glass. With a single, terrifying swipe of its massive claw, it swatted a Repterian frigate out of the sky as if it were a toy, tearing the metal hull to shreds.

The war between the Aquarians and Repterians suddenly shrank to insignificance.

I looked down at the glowing blue metal of the Trident in my hands. A heavy, sickening realization hit me. By disrupting Ayin's signal, had I acted as a beacon? Had I unleashed a force that threatened to consume us all?

Chapter 21: A Truce of Terror

The chaotic, overlapping shouts on the unencrypted comms abruptly died. It wasn't a tactical pause; it was the absolute, suffocating silence of two warring armadas simultaneously holding their breath.

"All units." Chief Drazil's voice rattled our speakers. The arrogant thunder was completely gone from his tone, replaced by the gritty, primal instinct of an apex predator staring up at a god. "Cease inter-faction hostilities. All batteries, re-target the leviathan."

A second later, Thalassa's cold, imperial frequency bled into the channel, her voice tight with strained urgency. "All Aquarian grids... coordinate with the Repterian fleet. Concentrate fire on the anomaly. May the ancestors have mercy on us all."

It was a truce forged in absolute terror.

Chaos gripped the yoke of the Arkenon, his knuckles stark white against his golden gauntlets. "Alright, team," he barked over our internal comms. "The schoolyard scuffle is over. Brace for the real fight."

The bruised sky violently ignited. Thousands of superheated Repterian plasma bolts and blinding Aquarian defense lasers stopped crisscrossing the ocean and converged onto a single, colossal point. The combined, apocalyptic firepower of two nations slammed into the beast.

But the sky didn't burn it. The energy washed over the leviathan, bending and dispersing inches from its stone scales.

"The hide is too thick!" Gex roared over the comms, staring at the tactical monitors in the cargo bay. "Conventional weapons are having zero effect!"

"It's not just the scales!" Poizen yelled, her fingers flying across the sensor readouts. "It's radiating an adaptive bio-energetic membrane! It's dispersing the kinetic impact before it even touches the armor!"

The serpent retaliated. It didn't roar; it simply moved. With a single, casual sweep of its colossal arm, its scythe-like claws effortlessly cleaved two Repterian dreadnoughts in half. The ruined, burning husks of the massive warships plummeted into the sea. The beast then shifted its weight, driving its lower half into the ocean. Millions of tons of water violently displaced, forming a towering, devastating tidal wave that rushed blindly toward the coastal shoreline.

"We need a new vector!" Kameel hissed. "It has to have a weak point!"

"Then we get closer," Chaos snarled, slamming the thrusters forward.

The Arkenon went into a steep, stomach-dropping dive. G-force pinned me against the co-pilot seat. "Lochlan, Kameel, splice into Drazil's comms!" I commanded, my golden gauntlets strangling the grip of the Tidal Trident. "Coordinate the fleet! Have them concentrate fire on its crown. Blind it! Draw its attention upward!"

We became a hornet buzzing around a titan. Chaos piloted with terrifying, reckless fluidity, barrel-rolling through the erratic crossfire of our own allies to avoid the serpent's thrashing limbs. I channeled my energy directly into the Trident, firing concentrated, cosmic blue shockwaves directly at the beast's glowing red eyes. The kinetic blasts made it flinch, but the bio-membrane absorbed the lethal damage.

The serpent reared back, its massive jaws unhinging.

A blinding, deafening torrent of necrotic, black energy erupted from its throat, cutting across the sky and instantly vaporizing an entire Aquarian defense platform.

"There!" Leon shouted over the comms, his voice cracking. "Watch its telemetry! The bio-field drops right after it purges that breath weapon! It's sluggish!"

"He's right!" Poizen yelled, throwing a thermal overlay onto the main viewport. "Beneath the jaw! The overlapping scales on its throat are glowing white-hot to vent the internal heat. It’s a thermal exhaust!"

It was a window. A fraction of a second, completely unprotected. And it required flying directly into the monster's unhinged jaw.

I looked at the thermal map, the heavy, sinking weight of reality settling into my bones. "We don't need to risk six lives for a one-shot run," I said, my voice dead-level over the comms. "Chaos and I are taking the shot alone. We need to get point-blank."

Chaos didn't argue. He understood the tactical math. "Drazil's flagship still has the heaviest shields in the armada," he said, pulling the yoke hard to port. "It's your best chance for survival. Hold on."

The Arkenon tore through the sky, matching speeds with the heavily damaged, smoking hull of the Repterian dreadnought.

The transfer was a frantic, deafening blur. I slammed the blast doors open. The howling ocean wind and the concussive shockwaves of the ongoing battle ripped through the cargo bay. Chaos hovered the

Arkenon mere feet from the flagship's exterior landing deck.

"Go!" I screamed over the wind.

Gex didn't hesitate, hurling his massive, scarred frame across the gap and hitting the dreadnought's deck with a heavy roll. "Give 'em hell, Theians!" he roared back.

Poizen and Leon vaulted across the divide with effortless, predatory grace. Lochlan hesitated on the edge of the ramp, his pale hands gripping the bulkhead as he looked back at me. "Don't do anything stupid, Gaia."

"No promises," I yelled back.

Kameel was the last to jump. Before he leaped into the wind, he placed a scaled hand flat against his chest, dipping his head in a deep, absolute gesture of Repterian respect. "May your strikes be true."

He jumped. I hit the console, and the heavy blast doors slammed shut, instantly severing the deafening roar of the war outside.

The sudden quiet of the pressurized cabin was heavy. It was just me, Chaos, the hum of the ship's engines, and the apocalyptic shadow of the leviathan filling the viewport glass.

Chaos locked the Arkenon into a predatory hover, his hands gripping the controls. He didn't look at me, his dark eyes fixed on the burning red eyes of the beast. "Just you and me now," he said, his voice dropping to a quiet, steady rumble. "Like the old times."

I looked down at the glowing blue metal of the Tidal Trident, feeling the Spirit Crystal pulse in my other hand. The odds were a statistical impossibility. The beast was a mountain. But the suffocating fear was gone, burned away by the raw, kinetic energy thrumming through my golden armor.

"Line up the shot," I said, stepping up to the viewport.

With the weight of a dying world on our shoulders, Chaos slammed the thrusters, and we flew directly into the jaws of the storm.

Chapter 22: The Price of Divinity

The Arkenon was a defiant gnat buzzing against a mountain of stone scales.

Below us, the united, apocalyptic firepower of the Repterian and Aquarian armadas washed over the leviathan like rain against stone. The beast didn't bleed; it simply absorbed the energy, a raging, primal force of nature completely immune to conventional war.

"It's not breaking the membrane!" Chaos roared over the deafening mechanical scream of our overtaxed thrusters. He violently threw the yoke to starboard, weaving the Arkenon through a chaotic web of stray plasma blasts and displaced ocean water. His knuckles were bone-white against his golden gauntlets. "We can't even scratch it!"

I didn't answer. I stepped up to the cracked viewport, gripping the Tidal Trident in my right hand. The divine, blue metal vibrated violently against my palm, a heavy, cosmic heartbeat. Strapped across my back, my wooden staff answered the call. Azrael’s Spirit Crystal pulsed in a rapid, sympathetic rhythm, radiating a strange, freezing heat through my golden breastplate.

I didn't just aim the weapon; I forced my will into the conductive metal, locking my eyes onto the glowing thermal exhaust beneath the serpent’s massive jaw.

I pulled the kinetic tether tight and unleashed the blast.

A beam of pure, condensed cosmic energy tore across the sky, slamming directly into the exposed, white-hot scales.

The beast recoiled. Its shriek didn't just tear through the air; the sheer acoustic force of the sound shattered the Arkenon’s remaining sensory arrays in a shower of sparks. A direct hit. But the monster didn't fall. The shriek twisted into a guttural, vibrating rumble of absolute fury.

Its colossal head, easily four times the size of our entire vessel, snapped downward. The ocean water cascading off its fangs mirrored the flashing emergency lights of our cockpit. Twin suns of malevolent, burning red locked directly onto the Arkenon.

"Gaia!" Chaos barked, banking the ship into a desperate evasive dive. "It's tracking us!"

I tried to pull the Trident back, but the weapon wouldn't move.

The blue light radiating from the prongs grew blinding, escalating into a violent, uncontrolled flare. Against my spine, the Spirit Crystal flared in unison, emitting an ethereal, piercing white light that reflected off the cockpit glass. The two artifacts were caught in a catastrophic resonance loop, feeding not just on my energy, but actively drinking in the immense, primal radiation pouring off the serpent outside.

"I can't cut the connection!" I grunted, my boots sliding against the deck plating as I tried to physically wrench the weapon downward. The golden metal of my gauntlets was growing blisteringly hot. "It's feeding on the leviathan!"

The air pressure inside the cabin spiked. The oxygen tasted like battery acid and raw ozone. A high-pitched, localized whine began to scream from the Arkenon's navigation console—the sound of shielding and gyroscopes being pushed past their physical breaking point.

Outside the shattered viewport, space itself began to warp.

The bruised horizon fractured. The boiling ocean, the smoke-choked sky, and the distant, warring fleets didn't just blur; they folded inward. The atmosphere tore open, pulled down an invisible drain into a kaleidoscopic, violently swirling vortex of prismatic light.

The serpent froze, its massive jaws snapping shut as the gravitational pull of the anomaly warped the water around it.

But it was too late for us. The Arkenon's thrusters screamed, whining in total mechanical failure as the vortex latched onto our hull with an irresistible, crushing magnetism.

"Hold on!" Chaos roared, his boots braced against the console as he physically fought the dead yoke.

But the ship was no longer flying. We were falling.

A final, blinding wave of absolute white light swallowed the cockpit. The deafening roar of the war, the shriek of the serpent, and the frantic alarms of our ship were instantly violently erased by a sudden, suffocating vacuum of silence.

Gravity ceased to exist.

There was only the sickening, weightless sensation of being ripped apart at a molecular level and aggressively stitched back together. My stomach vaulted into my throat. The breath was stolen from my lungs.

When the violent, agonizing tumbling finally snapped to a halt, gravity slammed back into me like a physical wall.

I hit the cold, unyielding deck plating face-first. The impact rattled my teeth. The Arkenon's emergency lighting flickered weakly, casting long, erratic shadows across the dead, silent bridge.

My vision swam in dark, unfocused waves. I dragged my heavy, unresponsive arm across the floor, my fingers blindly searching until they brushed the cooling, dormant metal of the Tidal Trident.

As the edges of my consciousness began to fray and pull me into the black, a terrifying, icy realization pierced the fog in my mind.

The Trident hadn't malfunctioned. It was a key. Was this the weapon's true power... or did the sorceress just pull us exactly where she wanted us?

The dark rushed in, and I surrendered to the silence.

www.ingramcontent.com/pod-product-compliance
Lightning Source LLC
Chambersburg PA
CBHW010321140726
48132CB00034B/498